DEDICATION

This book is dedicated to my mum Abigail
for her painstaking patience. It is also
dedicated to my siblings for their support, to
the interestingly wonderful people I have
been fortunate enough to meet over the
years, prior and whilst writing this book.
They have provided founding inspiration
for the content and material. Lastly, I would
like to dedicate this book to the ones I have
been fortunate to have loved, befriended
and lost.

The People We Meet (*T.P.W.M*)

Contents:

ACKNOWLEDGMENTS

Firstly, I would like to extend a huge thank you to my editor Hayden Cox for his professionalism, his acceptance to work with me on my first book, and his unceasing empathy. As without it, this book would not have materialized to a readable state. I would like to say a big thank you to Shabir Jogee for sharing such an amazing story on *New Years Eve of 2016*. His true story inspired an avalanche of fictional stories encapsulated in this book.

A simple thank you would be to burke the moment we met in *Kuala Lumpur*, how magical a converse we shared. Your insight truly helped with the final pick for this book's cover art my dearest friend Alissa Wedler.

Finally, it would be a crime if I did leave out my friends Carlos Queiros and Pablo Portabales for they provided the drive for me to pull through the painstaking effort needed to write a book. They provided an environment for a discuss that birth the existence of *T.P.W.M.*

Chapter 1

Arrival:

18:14 pm Saturday: Incheon International Airport,
South Korea 2015, so here we've flown 677 miles
from Beijing to South Korea.

Classic passenger "I need to be off the plane first"
syndrome: I couldn't help but wonder how everyone
thought they could, by some miraculous way, skip,
hop, or jump their way over fellow passengers
hoarded in front, all in a rush to get off the plane. At
this point, I reminded myself to stay calm and
breathe, which read like something off an early
British World War II memorabilia poster. What is
there to be gained by the self-inflicted pain of
impatience?

Like every new trip, I glanced around the plane and took in the views whilst we boarded and did the same whilst we disembarked. I checked out the sort of people that took the same journey as myself. What sort of people would be traveling from Beijing to South Korea? What sort of people visited South Korea, especially this time of year? It was September 5th, 2015. Were they just as exhausted?

All just pointless, aimless thoughts in my mind, a second later, they would have all been forgotten and I would try to remind myself of what was so important moments before.

What did I have in mind before I began such seamless, wool gathering, mind-surf that it had left me so brain vacant at the moment?

The middle-aged man had to get up again! I suppose this time there is a valid reason. He reached for the upper luggage compartment. He rummaged around it. The last time, it had been to retrieve a small case, mid-take off. Now, it's a jumper!

Excuse me, sir! Please, can you take a sit? We are about to land. One of the Cathy Airline hostesses rushed over in a haste to tend to him.

I'll help you with that. She suggested.

She quickly replaced the small bag back into the cluttered compartment it once came from, wedged tightly between other plastic bags labelled *duty-free*. Her sharp, white smile flooded in to put the man at ease.

The captiveness of the place, Aniko rattled on about how she would love to move to the city some day. It had left her thirsting for more. Nursing a terrible withdrawal for weeks on end. I am pretty sure we will all be getting off the plane soon. She said. There will be plenty of time for jumper searches, hinting at her frustration, which was easy to empathize with.

Her seat, *K19* was right next to mine, *K20*. I walked the narrow aisle on board, noticing how fortunately chosen the middle row seat had been close to an emergency exit. In the past, it would have been a missioned pursuit, one to avoid. I used to browse for hours to ensure the best window seat was selected and secured on booking, but on this occasion, I was left with little choice in the matter. The flight had been full. There was only a handful of seats left, reserved for an emergency. It didn't help that I had left it 'till the last minute.

On check-in, I paid the extra levy that would have gone down well on some lunch.
On board, the hostess was nonetheless helpful. She dismissively waved my paper itinerary and almost sent it flying across the counter. Cathay Pacific flight CA972 and seat K20 She said. It is near to emergency exit!

You might have to move out of the way in a case of an emergency. She said. All luggage has to be stored in the upper compartment, no luggage allowed on the floor! She said.

Aniko slouched into the slim-lined cloth upholstery 28 minutes in. She lifted her large tortoiseshell frame to exercise her eyes at times. The frame covered most of her face. It made it difficult to see just how emerald green her eyes really were. Behind those reading glasses, she winced and battered. At first, it was difficult to say whether or not she wanted me there. Two well-woven boxer braids fell comfortably on her shoulders. She twisted and turned them whenever she got bored, which seemed to be every two minutes. That got more frequent an hour or so into the flight.

If you were clever about doing some research and spending, you could drum up some pretty

impressive deals. My flight only cost me 21 US dollars, that's an equivalent if I convert from Hungarian Forints. She said.

She leaned over and spoke subtly. I make a good point of conveying as little as possible, she said. I would have to trust you to tell you, and oh, I would kill you if you told anyone. I'm not kidding. She said.

It was as though she guarded her tips as though they were some treasured gems. There are too many tourists these days. They ruin the magic of travel for me. She said. You really can't get as remote as you want these days. She added. Everyone's done it or knows about it.

A journey, traveling through South East Asia to discover another world, to go as remote as one's sore foot could possible carry. This was one of those connections with people on transit somewhere — someplace. At times, they led somewhere tangible. At times, they ended up nowhere tangible. At times, they were unique, somewhat special, encounters. Ours had been the latter — the sort that leaves one, feeling refreshed in the human experience. A sudden realization so sternly conceptualised, that there were people out there that had shared the same interest, outlook on culture, language, and a keen, almost committed pursual in seeing as much of south-east Asia as I had done.

I walked through crowds of Chinese, Filipino, Japanese tourists, Korean returnees, and a few western faces. I felt a strong sense of familiarity, the same perceived from every transpacific/transatlantic international terminal so far, yet this time, I felt a tingle of excitement knowing this was completely new terrain, an entirely new country from the one just visited with a whole new way of thinking, with new culture, food, and philosophy.

Standing with most of his back to a pillar, his hands tucked deep into the pockets of his straight cut jeans, he seemed to wear them as though he were frightened they would drag to the floor. He managed to occasionally make eye contact. It was like chasing a goldfinch. He smiled, his lips slightly smacked together in a semi-arch. You just about got the feeling he restrained from a conversation.

Is this your first time in Korea?

In a strong German accent, he enquired.

Are you also here for the Exchange Program?

Well... No, I am traveling through Asia. I responded.

Oh, that's sort of pretty cool. He went on.

The German Student liked being referred to as "Pat."
He was from a small fishing town close to Hamburg.
A number of worn out stringed bracelets noticeably
graced his wrist; they looked like he had worn them
over a long period of time due to their exposure to
the sun. A very recognizable band stood out. One
inscribed with the words:

''Segle wie der wind.''

Two Polaroids fell out of his notepad, narrowly
missing his gaze. They scattered frivolously over the
polished floors. He carried on talking, oblivious to
his lost prints about to be trampled upon.

Attentively, he sifted through for his itinerary as
Aniko reached to help pick up the two fallow prints
from the floor and slip them back into his folder.

Oh, thanks! He responded, only just catching sight of
her alacrity.

The Polariods were out on the floor long enough to
make out the sketchy images. They looked like prints
of friends having a good laugh at the snap of the
camera.

A Polaroid camera hung from his neck. He wisped through his folder and more Polaroids could be seen loosely packed within the pages of cut news briefings.

This was his first trip to South Korea. He made mention.

At first, I wasn't sure what to expect. He said.

His strong native dialect bumbled along as an undercurrent beneath his English.
As minutes flew by he seemed to unravel more and more out of his shell. Quite an unusual chap, unlike the many other travellers. The ones Aniko passionately loathed, the ones interested and vested, only in their own self-importance. with no regards for locals even less regards for country. Keen to get on with whatever next chapter of an adventure they had lined up.

Aniko leaned over, wanting to be part of the conversation. In an almost journalistic manner, she engaged, holding up her mobile phone just below her lips, adjusting her tortoise-rimmed glasses, and Pat was all too eager to disclose more.

International relations!

Oh, well, it is a very broad subject to study, Pat said.

A lot to do with social economics and communications. He said. I really got into it as I am interested in other peoples' culture, although I am not sure what I will do when I finish studying it. he added.

Well, most people don't know what they want to do when they finish studying, so its okay! Aniko remarked.

He rambled on at a pace and enthusiasm only a twenty-something would bother to adopt.

Never been to Asia before.

He went on.

It's very different from Germany.

He went on.

This particular trip was somewhat eye opening to me, a culture shock! He bumbled, his German accent an undercurrent beneath his English.

He drank from his 1-liter water bottle, his face strained with anxiety as he uncapped and sipped from the narrow bottleneck.

I wonder why he is so nervous when there is no reason to be. What is the worst that can go wrong?

Standing in front of Carousel A23/24, arrival from Beijing *18:14 pm* local time. A chime is heard from the far right of the conveyer belt. Then, a few yards of empty rollers transited past the crowd of now eagerly waiting passengers. One black mid-sized suitcase came out first. Then several others of different sizes and colours. I spotted my equally mid-sized black TULLY suitcase headed towards our side of the crowd and made ahead for it. It had been ruffled, experienced a degree of fatigue similar to the printed itinerary.

I pulled, lifted, and motioned my case off the Carousel and through the crowd. I raised an eyebrow to Pat and said my goodbyes.

All the best with your studies, mate! All the best for your trip!

Pat replied. A brief encounter, I thought to myself, one not leading anywhere!

Aniko tagged along and we both walked through the crowded luggage collection area. One TULLY suitcase and a backpack, *the KEG* strapped to my back. She had a large barrel bag hinged on wheels that she dragged along with her silver backpack, also strapped to her back. As soon as we passed through the *Nothing to declare,* sign above. I yanked out the Old Oliver and started to slide through my song list.

Something that captures the moment, I thought!

I decided on So What" by Miles Davis — a kind of blues album.

In the far distance, there was the same middle-aged man meeting a slender lady at the exit of the arrival foyer. She was Korean, must have been either his wife or maybe a girlfriend. Either way, she seemed really pleased to see him, giving him a big kiss, which she landed right on his lips. He held her by her slender frame and immediately, the feeling of jealousy filled me.

Aniko looked over. She had seen me pull out the silver media player, the one I called Old Oliver.

You're not planning on listening to that now, are you? she said. *Old Oliver*, she teased. I wonder who gave names to their stuff? She said. It is just a bit weird. She said. Wait a minute! You wouldn't get it. It's my thing, been my thing for quite a long while now."

I tucked the small music player into my top right pocket. "*Old Oliver*," you would think. What a name for a piece of surmountable steel.

She had wanted to share a cab into town, but we were headed in opposite directions. She was headed for Busan, a southern part of the south, whilst I was headed for central Seoul.

We talked about an exchange of contact details, a way to stay in touch whilst we both navigated in separate directions across the Korean peninsula. A social media platform perhaps. She suggested.

You can get me on here, best to wait until you get some reception. I suggested.

Okay, I have added you! You're on my friend's list. Let me know how your trip goes. She responded.

It has been one of my favourite places to visit whilst being here. she added.

We hugged, and she held on a second or two longer.

Keep in touch, right. She suggested.

The black digital controller was already on Miles Davis's "*Kind of Blue*" album. I tapped on its circular middle button and it released a stream of music into my ears, so welcoming, as if going back to a time when the compulsive need to explore came upon me.

I became a new listener to Jazz music the year before. It was like discovering a lost treasure right on the shores of the Kynance. Stumbling upon a precious metal, aged and tarnished on the coastal lines of Cornwall like discovering that quaint Jazz club found in the midst of the antics shops near questionable establishments in Koln's Diggy bars area. I was lost, only to discover a new love as old and tarnished, a new love for Jazz, a Coltrane piece called "A Love Supreme".

I closed my eyes and imagined seeing the needle gliding nonchalantly over the waxed record, finding the rhythms within the grooves and streaming its beautiful melodies. It's travelling pace almost like musical notes raced off the top of a vinyl as I imagined. This got my mind in gear, a sort of calm state with an insane capability to organize or coordinate. Any task at hand felt easier in that moment as the music imparted a calming auditory whilst I listened. This time, I walked round Incheon's massive airport, feeling less lost within the enormous modern construction.

I exited the main arrival arch and entered through a large shopping foyer. I am in Korea! The thought jumped through the cloud of emptiness as I listened to the distancing composition.

I am surrounded by Korean calligraphy and it is on everything!

A feeling of excitement, an apprehension, and a slight sense of being lost in the ambience of it all!

Nari smiled with refreshing vigour Kamsamida, as easy as she said it as easy as it would have been forgotten so I repeated quietly several times over Kamsamida!" "Kamsamida!

She returned back to her typing as promptly as she had responded. The glared monitor adorned in front of her cast a bright shade of hue, cyclic as she worked away on its keys. My attempt at being friendlier had come as a surprise to me too.

The pull from the glare of the monitor seemed stronger. Those happy eyes soon disappeared, lost within the hue it seduced.

The foyer quickly got busier with an outpour of arriving passengers. Many who had recently been re-acquainted with their luggage made their way towards Nari the information attendant.

I motioned down the escalators towards the direction of the ATM she had mentioned, exited out Incheon airport, and was hit by the humid Korean heat, which dazzled over my face.

"It hot here, brilliant!"

''I certainly won't be needing this jacket of mine, as I would back home.'' I took off my jacket and folded it away.

I took in the views. The beautifully designed airport architecture looked amazingly stunning both inside and outside. I looked back through the automatic sliding door and its large see-through glass panes.

Another thought jumped out at me as I headed towards the AREX express rail bound for Seoul Central station.

''*Everything seems so well organized here.*''

Chapter 2

The Meet:

Manchester England 2014- February; Papers to an up coming exam were scattered across the bistro table, I am in much need for a refresher. It is the afternoon of a wet chilly Manchester's summer day. Traffic is light with the usual regulars and I am spitting for a coffee.

Eagle-eyed, I watched the barista as she handed me a black coffee. The tension from contemplating the forthcoming exams in a fortnight sent chills down my spine. It's not my strongest module. The fidgeting took a toll and this became a lot more apparent.

I was nervous, it had been clear but I couldn't decipher whether it was about the papers or the girl, the one whom I met only once before and was about to walk through those wide doors any minute.

I felt the stiffness as I attempted to move my neck in the opposite direction to see if she was coming, Minutes had passed, too slowly for my liking, these papers scattered on the bistro table in front made less and less sense, the more I stared. I had hoped she would walk in soon and save me from them, save me from the misery of the pursuit to make sense of these drifting texts.

The daylight would be a better option, better to set eyes on her in the clear light of day. The weariness sets in, it had been a long dull morning. Is she as she was in the dark? The thought lingered. The lights could have been deceiving the way they had hit her eyes and made them sparkle. Intermittently her eyes, illuminated every time she tilted her head from one side to the other. Her glossy fresh-face radiated such youthfulness, such beauty in the dark as much as the dim light would allow to be captured.

My eyes offered a blurry vision, fatigued from the dancing in the midst of the dark crowded room. The weakness in alcohol drove my tongue dry from the booze served. Cheap to pull in the young crowd, I drank with a little kick from the alcohol strength, a cold glass of water would have been better, the thought loomed through the thick of my mind, stood there in midst of the bustling crowd watching her dance the showery night away.

Bottled beers sat comfortable in huge blocks of ice behind the bar counter, they had made their peak once more the moment Jason had placed his order. It was his turn with the rounds, his back to the jubilant crowd, head high almost kissing with the ceiling, I could see him from where I stood pressed amongst the bodies talking to the whiskered bar tender, all of 6ft 2 inch of him, towering over the mass.

The bartender handed over the first bottle and then three more, the fifth and sixth followed right after. Jason easily passed each bottle from the whiskered bartender's cold hands to Oma and then myself, all six bottles until each person had at least two bottles, the last one reached my hands warm from the transit. Oma wasn't pleased with beer either.

Good Heavens, they could do with a chiller back there. Oma mentioned. We cheered to the warm beers and I nodded to thank Jason, a sort of cool acknowledgment of a good deed soon enough to be repaid.

We attended the same lectures" Professor Agata's Quantum Physics Modules I and II. Although, Jason seemed to weather those storms better than we did.

We played a game of six degrees of separation and was sure Jason was in some way or another connected to almost everyone at the club. Any given moment he could be swept away by the young clammering crowd.

What was his charm?

I remembered my first meeting with him, shooting a cue stick at the clubhouse, south of the city, a place frequented by the dodgy archetype. It pulled us in with cheap beer and fruit machines on site.

His loud gregarious voice could be heard from the entrance even before we pushed open the door.

Oma, an expert at diversion, evaded whenever Jason directed his famous rant. He always went on about nothing. You could have heard him a mile off, adrift in a slur of words, all of which irritated me.

Back at the coffee house she straddled in. It looked like she had just been chased by a rabid dog.

Sorry I was late. I was helping a friend move. She just signed a new lease. She said.

Her fidget was new, her eyes dotted about the room as if to catch a gaze of someone she expected to be there.

Those damn boxes! They cut me!

Her smile was something more of a mystery,
more of a smirk, like a little lie, she secretly hid well,
carefully guarded from peering eyes. She ran her
hands through her hair constantly but there was
nothing wrong with it.

A little-known fact was, we met only a week ago at the club, the dimly lit room allowed only a fraction of light through. Only a fraction of her beauty was captured.

The top right window seemed to be of significant interest to her. She constantly glanced at it, that old basement of the university's central archive. It had new life breathed into it, now it staged as a student café.

It had not been open long. Fresh wet paint replaced the smell of old damp that got really bad on rainy days. Manchester, a city so well accustomed to heavy greys, wet trouser patches meant, that one almost had to live in willies.

Underneath the basement, that acrid sipped right through it's bad water drainage and created its infamous damp atmosphere, eerie as a result of bad lighting even at daytime. This added to its ambiance.

That old space, she wouldn't have dare entered months before, was now an artsy café and she sat right in the middle of it in her red puffer, like a spot of Ox blood dropped in the middle of a white sheet of paper.

Of what significance were the large barn windows to her? She would reverse jettison, sat beneath those large barn frame. Her eyes constantly dotted and followed every shadow that wandered above.

This time artsy fashionistas frequented the place rather than bookworms and intellects that braved the dark, their noses held shut to minimize the hit from the acrid.

"So, did you have a good night Monday?"

The last forty minutes had gone like good cheese on biscuit. Each time she referred to just how popular the night was with the crowd.

"All this free time, I found it really difficult to harness!"

—

20

She referred to making time for her studies. She went on about her friends, where she had met them, and how lucky she was to have them.

"Lynette and I met at Fresher's." She went on.

Her eyes dotted for the barn windows, the shadows that lingered above, each passing stranger seemed a target to be spotted.

"Yes 'em! Well we were… both in line for the ladies hockey team."

Again her eyes dotted for yet another inconspicuous shadow.

"We clicked instantly and Sophie, we met at this very coffee shop two weeks ago."

The scattered papers that covered the bistro table divided us. I wanted to throw them aside and just get right to her. This would be the third time the thought had kissed my cortex and it seemed well spirited with the idea, each time it sent a shiver of apprehension down my spine.

Will the nettling of bees ever happen? How far would it go? Before she figures out, it had all been a scam?

She went on:

Turns out we shared the same taste in Lululemon. What do you know? She chuckled hard.

She glanced at the top right window, two weaved characters stood there and peered in, down through the glass slit above the large barn windows. Their hourglass silhouette gave away that they were both females.

Did they know her? Could they have also come along with her?

She chuckled as she realized the bewilderment on my face. She had been caught red-handed. Both of her friends had stood adjacent to the large barn window outside and peered in through its opened upper slit to observed and assess how this first meeting was going.

It had the better of me as I pondered over what she might have said before she made her entry and gingerly sat in the bistro chair. Her bushy eyebrow rose in an instant as she wittily sneaked to take another quick glance at the large pane windows to the right of us.

Back to that very moment, the night before, when she barged into me. A small centimetre radius where we had danced, all of which lasted a total of 40 minutes and then her speedy getaway.
They had been looking for her the whole night, apparently! Now there she sat, gingerly across the table from me, a supposedly stranger.

———

So, what are you like? She asked. I had expected some sort of quiz. This hardly threw me off. I knew for certain she had been burning to once again hand me a barrage of an intrusive line of questioning.

So, who were you out with that night?

She took another glance at the far right window and this time she giggled real hard and out of place!

She is really bad at this espionage thing! I thought to myself.

Such a bad giveaway, I thought.

It was almost like she wanted to be caught. She wanted me to know we were being watched.

That wooden sound from the bistro chair dragged against the concrete floor. Cold and abrupt as she pulled at it, the other sound was longer and screeched as the other girl had pushed to make space as she sat down, both were unhappy about something or someone, they had both settled right behind us. Melanie's chuckling grew louder as she heard the racket happening behind.

My guess was they knew her and wanted to listen in.

So what is it you're studying? She asked as she pulled at one of the paper in front of her. She examined it only loosely and then lousily displaced it back where it dropped onto pile of other scattered papers on the bistro.

This was my opportunity to really drive the conversation and take charge. The girls behind us knew her. Perhaps they were the waiting shadows she glanced at ever so dottily.

Nothing was wrong with her hair but she still toyed at it. It became more progressive the longer she sat there. I wasn't particularly impressed by her levity or her gained sense of enjoyment, some sense of joy she acquired riffling her paws through cottons that was my amore.

Well, I did tell you.

Ha! Right. Art and Design.

That's what she studied, another artsy one. I am in her territory, in the midst of others just like her, and I stood out like a vibrant highlight on one of Picasso's cubism piece.

That Art deco painting pinned to the wall at the bar where we had danced. I remembered our conversation so vividly. She spoke of painting so candidly before I had asked for her hand and whisked her to the floor. It was painting of a lady in a red dress in towering heels dancing the tango. It had hung centred on the wall above a leather sofa where the young patron chatted away obliviously beneath it.

It's such a bold painting! It reminds me of a lot of Dali, the way that she has been painted. Such muscular features for a woman, a lot stronger than her male partner.
Just look at the strain on his face, he is really struggling to lead her. She said.

She is one strong woman! I added. The painting hung and we watched, motionless whilst the pulse of the crowd went hard as we stood at the club.

Well, Quantum Physics! What's that even for? asked Melanie. She brought me back to the café, her curiosity intensified as she stared at the scribbled notes on one the paper.

Nanoscale analysis of atoms... What's all this sciency stuff? She asked.

Okay I don't get it! She asked again. The paper fell loosely as quickly as it had been displaced.

Well, It's my final year and I really ought to get my head down for this. I replied. It's quantum physics, my third year in. I added.

Okay! Smartass! Where is the name from? She asked.

Is it Ivory Coast? She blurted.

Ray DeCosta, my name clearly drafted on the top right section of the folder placed to the side on the bistro table.

It's actually Ghanaian but close enough. I replied.
Have you been to Africa before?

Arrogant Melanie was subdued and a much more
empathetic one emerged within seconds. She pushed
ahead, lunged forward as if to get closer, a few
meters from my face.

You see, I love Africa! I love it passionately so. She
said.
How is it you love it that passionately? I said in
response. The sudden change in her grammar came
as a slight surprise.

My papa was born in Africa, in Malawi. she said as
she candidly observed the massive contrast between
both our faces. Hers, pale white against my ebony
dark, her smirk was back, taken by the vast contrast.

She went on. Summer '07, Papa had always wanted
me to experience a bit of the thrill of freedom he
experienced growing up in Africa. He encouraged it
strongly, although mama wasn't so keen about me
going to Africa.

Chad Elephant Sanctuary was my solace. I remember it
fondly now.
I was at a cross roads with life at the time. I had lost
something dear to me… someone.

Hmmm… autonomously I extruded, from the
bottom of my gut in empathy, like a firefly caught in
sticky ointment, surrendered to whatever fate might
follow.

She went on, such magnificent animals! Poaching went on a lot in this part of Central Africa. She said.

I am well aware of this. It still goes on today. I said.

Elephants are still being preyed on for precious Ivory. It's so sad. She said.

Her sentiment had hit hard, hard enough that I shared in the angst. She wore it across her face as broad as a canvass. That same sentiment had struggled hard to mask her youthful beauty.

What came upon me was a strong reticent familiarity. *Only before we were total strangers*. We met at the club, the dim lit venue allowed only a fraction of her beauty to me. Now she was at the bistro table across from me. *Not a stranger anymore. Not a friend either*. It felt like I had known her the entirety of my life.

Was this good? Was this bad? Or maybe I suddenly developed a bit soft spot?

That wooden elephant figurine, it all made better sense now. That key ring that held it together with other keys, that opened doors to places she rented.

This wooden elephant I have had this since Chad. She said. It had emerged from the cluster of keys placed on the bistro table close to the scattered papers on quantum science and I had only noticed it when she toyed with the keys.

You know about 80% of the Ivory sold on the black market comes from African elephant. Its pretty shocking what these people do to those beautiful elephants.

She was knowledgeable….

Cameroun is French-speaking isn't it? So I found it a bit difficult as my French isn't at all great. She said.

Growing up in Ivory Coast, I spoke French. I don't speak a lot of it now and I mess up as I think the phrase in English. I said.

C'est assez commun. She said. The more you speak it, the more it stays with you. Melanie added.

She goes on…

There was this particular ranger at the park where we volunteered. Brice was his name, Once we went with him on his usual patrol of the park. This was near *N'Djamena*.

Caught in the middle of a raging stampede, the poor fella got the worst of it. Some poachers. As she had put it. Were making a bush leaguer attempt at the memory. Those juveniles were at the mother herd for her prized tusk, they had alerted the rest of the herd towards the lone automobile refuged amongst large *Baobab* trunks where we had parked to observe the herd. The ranger was on all fours, lurking to catch the juveniles when he got the brunt of the herd's charge towards him.

Stupid teenagers! She said.

Everyone gets taken advantage of down there. The poacher touts! They only get less than a hundred dollars for a tusk that sells for hundreds of thousands. She said.

The black market, it is a really frustrating business. She added.

Fake permits and the lot! She added.

It's a real mess really. Brice was lucky enough to escape with just a broken tibia. He had to be on crutches for months. She went on.
She heard the coughing that came from behind her. On cue she was at ease, hypnotic, as if taking a step back from it all.

Oh! Well I can't stay long I have to be somewhere now. It was nice to meet you again.

Her eyebrow sunk at an instant. She got up from the bistro and threw her hair backward…

It was nice to meet you too. I said.

She met her friends at the table behind.

This is Lynette and Sophie. Hey, meet Ray. She said.

I peered over Lynette and Sophie, both with wide smiles and a wave that came quickly afterwards, a sort of silence acknowledgement an approval won over.

Lynette showed off her sleeve almost immediately. She had very intricate floral ink that decorated her left arm all the way to her wrist. She was a very attractive blonde. Sat next to her was Sophie a petite brunette with classic features.

The more outspoken one of the group, opinionated yet punctilious, was Melanie.

We are going to head off for lunch now. It's been a long morning moving all of Lyn's things! Melanie stated.

She pushed the bistro table only slightly and stretched for an embrace, which I was only too glad to give to her. The sudden wet patch from her lips took me by surprise, leaving a cold sensation where her lips had been. She smelt of fresh morning rose the first time I noticed her scent.

My iris locked a target on her behind as she moved between the bistros to meet her friends, somewhat like a snake manoeuvre its way through a thick shrub. They all offered a wave goodbye. I am glued to the views of her behind, but I give a customary look at them all. For a brief moment, I found myself buried deep within the fluff of thoughts that rummaged in my mind. I was not lost in it, but cosy with desire to have her in my arms. *"Will the nettling of bees ever happen with her? Am certain she wants to see me again."*

Chapter 3

The Break:

Manchester 14- December 22nd
This isn't right. I've known it for a while. Deep down it didn't make any sense. What would have made it more vivid? Clear as crystal to me. Jason said.

She might be losing interest. Oma said.

Over the pool table, we would debate. The last time, she made a good excuse, turning up at the flat in the early hours.

Sorry, Lynette was sick. She said. She had too much to drink I had to stay with her, couldn't leave her side. Melanie insisted.

What sort of friend would that make me? She pushed.

If it wasn't that, it was the C.A.T.

Can't Answer That. Ne peut pas répondre à cela.'' In the minutest of French she spoke ,and she did to be clever.

Where were you last night? I asked Can't answer that. She responded.

I rang your phone and you wouldn't pick. Why was that? I asked Can't answer that! She responded.

Vraiment, ce n'est pas votre affaire She peltered some more French. Est-ce que tu vois quelqu'un d'autre ? Est-ce cet homme de l'Agence ? I asked.

I would raise hell and start an argument, she insulted mostly in French, it sounded much more better that way, much more effective.

Pourquoi ne peux-tu pas l'admettre? Petite putain!

Je vous aid it qu'il est juste un ami vous baise! She replied.

Ce vieux sac est ton ami? Pourquoi tu ne ecris pas juste stupide sur ma chienne de front! I said.

If that didn't work, I would try a softer and more subtle approach. Either way, she was much cleverer than me. Time grew between us. The distance grew even wider. Each night the cold patch between the sheets grew and got even colder. It's certain her heart had been stolen by another older, perhaps wiser fellow.

It had been 11 solid months having a good go at it, 11 months since that infamous meeting at the artsy café below the student library. One major holiday to Paris and 12 minor spats, one job change, two graduations, one funeral—her great auntie Beatty's—one wedding: Sophie's. Only the honeymoon period kept coming back. None of the mess just the good old six months of it.

That wild sex, every 708 times. The progressivity of it all. Insistently, she kept coming back for more of the same, regardless of commitments, regardless of social norms and regardless of the stigma. That steel black media player to which she loaded the songs we both enjoyed- Old Oliver, I named it after her thirst for more. Old, as if I had desperately wanted to distance myself from it all.

I was sure she had been the one for me. Or possibly, I am being delusional with only a numbered experience. I did not have a great deal to compare it too. Before now, the Sony gamer with the three knuckleheads across the globe, conversed through clunky headsets, was my solace. Those nasty trolls, the cursing, however revolting, humanized me from the cold barren confines of my room. They gave me connectivity.

Since the halt, it seemed my subconscious had re-concurringly anchored me to the past. It betrayed me, constantly and unconsciously led me back to the dark, abusive, and cold.

I don't want to go out today. Pouvons-nous rester dans? Melanie insisted.

They were the good old 182 nights. A good two weeks and I haven't set eyes on her. Her keys with the small elephant figurine seemed a thing of the past then, even though we had shared a flat. I started to feel like a stranger or a flatmate, at most.

Whenever the front door swung open, there would be some more arguments. I should have learnt by now there was no way I would come out triumphant, it's really not my strong suit.

The intimacy had long dissolved to as little as a note on the kitchen cabinet.

Could you get some milk, please? We ran out! Melanie's handwriting scribbled roughly on a yellow sticky note. That's if she wanted it to be cordial.

I sat and imagined ways to recapture the past as new. *What good gesture could I do? "Get back in her good books, back to the good old days, when things were just right."* I thought to myself.

"You have to rumble with the situation or you will fumble Stand up for yourself or get ran over!" That was one thought! Another, *"Let her go! That ship has sailed."*

Oma gave his two pennies worth, took a shot at a spotted green packed close to the padded borders of the table. The thinking came a lot clearer, easier this time, just like the certainty of that week's old milk gone bad. Actualising, on the other hand, required effort. A little strife! One I hadn't contemplated on.

The neediness buried deep down, it practically made my core. This, of course, was only observable to her.

You changed a lot! You're not the same guy I met. She said.

Covers blown like upskirts revealed a concealed peach, a front torn to bits like shreds. She was my totalitarian, self-absorbed, narcissistic mate. Do you love me?
She would insist. This was before the crash.

No one's immune. She said. I am not perfect either. She said. I guessed like a fair, well-sculptured porcelain pottery. You are hell bound to find some cracks if you bother to examine closely.

Here we were. Her affection quickly faded away like a fallen pack of cards to a stacked up tower. No magic trick could wind them back up. No magic trick could lure her back. Her ship unanchored months ago and I stood at the harbour watching it voyage these rough waters.

A dingy pool house south of the city flashed back at me, dimly lit to procure some emphasis. Humorously I recollected a time we had a good old row. I didn't speak for weeks, but miraculously managed to win her back. I guessed it was her favourite, the cream based mushroom risotto.

I would wisp until my hands were sore and over. I doused some common spices, the black pepper did a trick of black magic, splashed chardonnay for zest. Sadly, she had grown too accustomed to these tricks! The cats were out and there was no going back to them now. She did well to say her piece, well lack of it, more or less.

The cue stick struck a well-organised pyramid of balls and they scattered into a cluster. A number of stripes disappeared into the netted hole overseen by the dim-lit lamp that hung above the green board.

Oma and Jason went back and forth like a seesaw, a barrage of insult as I stood there watching their boyish contest. *Everyone bickers, its human nature*, I thought to myself, but when Melanie and I did it, it took a turn for the worse.

There were the many Agata's lectures on special relativity, quantum theory, most of which went over our heads, all three of us at a dingy old pool house south of city to escape the rigor.

Once, we both caught Jason snoring at an octave similar to that of a bleating calf, petrified at the thought of being perturbed. Of course, Oma was crafty enough to capture footage on his smartphone, heightened by the acoustics of the empty auditorium. We teased Jason with it and until today, he won't live it down.

I knew little of Oma but he seemed to assert himself well: a know it all man-god, lady killer. Sure, he had the looks, being from the Gulf and blessed with the natural charisma of a sheik, he would boast. Brother! Just let her go! You can get yourself another girl. Never stress over any woman, Never! You should trust me!

I was unsure if this was good advise. He didn't know Melanie. "He never met her. What does he know? He knows nothing of her quirkiness but maybe he has a point." I would go through the dialogue in my head. A pretty down right kind of guy I thought at the time.

I recollected dinners at Lynette and Sophie's. That student flat they both shared in the heart of the northern quarter a few miles from the box office where I used to work and the many dinners we had there.

Melanie had tried to get me to go along and I didn't particularly enjoy Lynette's cooking. She let her food linger for too long, most of it came out either tougher or soggier.

The chills of the quiet night comforted me reassuringly. It would have been just as painstakingly difficult to hang around. Best to let things be as they would. Forcing it would only lead to more pain, long and short of it, we broke up that night at Lynette's. I imagined it had all been a set up.

As I walked those steep hills of Garosugil with Eloise and the constant stream of Aniko's text that vibrated through my back pocket.

It didn't feel so bad then. A year had past and it was all behind me.

Back at the pool house, I watched Oma nonchalantly take a shot at a spotted blue. I wondered whether this was his attitude too — not caring too much about the outcome but effortlessly exerting himself with just the right amount of panache.

Maybe this was what was missing from my approach. The right balance of piquancy. I seemed to have lost mine. I focused so much on my fears. I honed onto them like a raging bull, doused with a flash of red fabric.

Finally it dawned on me. I had been chasing my whole life rather than seizing the moment and living it.

A shot at the cue ball and it paced at rapid speeds. It crashed directly into a small cluster of balls. I watched a stripe ball quickly disappear into the netted hole followed by another two spots, this left Oma in the lead of the game.

Yes brutha! Thanks a lot for that. You lucky Bagger!. Jason said.

I sized up the remaining balls on the green, just two spots left and three stripes packed further along the table belonging to Jason.

Oma placed his cue well balanced, anchored at an arch between his thumb and fourth finger. He took his shot, striking first at a spotted ball, and sent it right into the hole, adjacent to his opponent's striped balls.

That's how it's done!

He aimed to take his second, struck the white ball and sent it traveling in the direction of Jason's packed stripe, knocking two consecutively into the hole, changing the hand of the game.

Chapter 4

Guesthouse: Seoul

18:24 pm Brown Line 6 Gongdeok Seoul South Korea 2015.

I held the TULLY suitcase in-between my legs and sat on a crowded Metro Car. It headed towards downtown Itaewon. An obvious silence was observed as the car jittered along the track. To my right, an elderly Korean woman sat, well dressed in smart baggy trousers and matched lace top. Her black flat shoes were well worn. You could imagine these were her comfy go-to shoes as she reclined into the long lightly padded cloth upholstered seat, almost meditative in the state.

To my front was a young professional in a smart navy blue suit and light blue shirt, with an emerald green tie to match. The train stopped at Samgakiji Station. I couldn't help but notice how well above the ankles his trousers sat above his well-polished shoes, displaying his grey socks like some sort of treasured gem.

An equally smartly dressed young Korean lady entered the car and took the man's place. Tapping away on her Smartphone, she barely lifted up her head. Clenched by her side was a pricey-looking handbag that matched her shoes. A quick glance around the car and I observed everyone was pretty smartly dressed in the car with a few exceptions, including myself. The train travelled a few miles down the track to the next station and more people get on.

I reclined back into the padded seat. I looked up to observe my stop. *"Itaewon! Aha, it's the next one."* I thought to myself.

The train stopped at Itaewon station and I made my way up the long lengthy escalator, which must have been about 190ft below sea level. I wondered to myself.

"Why such a depth?"

It turns out the tube station doubled as bomb bunker just in case a bomb raid from the North was imminent. As the escalator ascended to the surface, some unusual adverts caught my eyes, of course, all in Korean. At first, it was difficult to make out exactly what they were trying to endorse.

Every few meters, ads popped up, rolled on papered screens, framed in such a way, each seamlessly displayed a spread on pharmaceuticals then K-pop, then electronics and so on, as I rode the lengthy elevator up.

I tapped the *City Pass*, the micro chipped barrier swung open at an instant. Some more foreign faces gathered at the foyer, students from the looks of them, North Americans from their west coast accents. A few more steps up the slated stairs and I am hit once again by the hot Korean breeze.

TULLY on toll, Kev the blue, strapped to my back and Old Oliver for entertainment. These old Aladdin's alley of stores bestowed upon us, coffee houses, K-pop clubs, Korean restaurants. The music was loud and brash. Google Maps was once again hopeless, constantly directed and re-directed in opposing ways.

How do people navigate around here?

The last time I was lost, I was deep in the Namtok Mae Tho Forest Chiang Rai northernmost part of Thailand. One minute before, I was making my way up a steep Gyeongnidan alley and the next, it sent me back down the same alley, caught in a frenzy, locals eyes feasted gaze at me.

That last 4 minutes, aimless circle of imaginary footprints, through a sparely deserted Gyeongnidan. My frustration started to build. The two young Koreans had been staring the whole time. Finally, they gathered some courage and walked up to me. Old Oliver still in hand, I stood toddlishly confused.

"Hey! Do you need some help?"

The pair enquired. They must have spotted me coming up the Metro, wandering the main stripe at Itaewon clearly like a tourist, which clearly was the case. Our paths had crossed once at the Manimal smokehouse and again at the intersection between Coffee Smith and Monster bar.

Yea! Sure I can do with some help. I responded back. I need to find the guesthouse hostel. I said.

He quickly grabbed TULLY from me and this shocked me at first.

Let me help you with that?

Min-Jae reservedly anchored to his side like symbiotic species, reliant on one another for survival. We walked a few minutes in absolute silence, enough for me to notice the local taverns starting, an afternoon solvent takings. She broke her silence soon afterwards.

Where are you from? Tae-Song asked.

Her English came with such eloquence, commanded well. Either she had lived abroad or learnt it from a native.

I am from England, Do you know it? I asked. 'Oh yes! Uh Um! He exclaimed.

Min-Jae recoiled her petite face to the side of Tae-Song's arm like a turtle recoiled back into its shell. Her petite frame stayed glued to his side as they wandered along with TULLY almost confiscated.

———

We really like Manchester United! Yes! We like Manchester. Tae-Song joined unison.

Well, that's where I am from. I added.

'Do you know Park? Park Ji-Sung! Tae-Song repeated.

Yes in fact I do. Played for Manchester United.

Yes! The best football player in the world!

Tae-Song added. Clearly an element of bias availability cascade with a good degree of confirmation.

Manchester, Good City.

He urged on, like a ship's captain at battle with an undeniable determination to sail through a siege cleverly laid ahead. I thought of Nelson.

Park! He played, for Manchester United, very long time! Hmm! Good player! The best! He went on.

There was no objection to his course of convention as Andrea Pirlo puts it.

'' *The midfielder must have been the first nuclear-powered South Korean in history. In the sense that he rushed about the pitch at the speed of an electron.''* [sic] I am with him on that point.

He adjusted the frame to his owl styled glasses almost mathematically. He wore them well, a cropped haircut bang covered his forehead. His pressed shirt was tucked firmly into his blue chino with loafers to match. It was almost as though a mannequin had just stepped out of a shop and walked the steep narrow lanes, imitating life as real. Every strand in place to his jet-black hair contrasted with his pale skin. With me to his left and it's like night and day walking the street of Gyeongnidan.''

"Guest House Hostel. That's where I have to be."

We headed back in the same direction up the alleyway. Tae-Song seemed to have a fair idea where it was, although he did never be there before. He had heard of the place. We passed by a number of Korean restaurants, taverns, adult stores, seedy brothels, and bathhouses.

It's like neon heaven here! The thought shoots through my mind, a kind of adult Disneyland.

"Yes, it's like this all the time."

Tae-Song caught this. I hadn't realized I had said it out loud. We motioned on.

We are out for the evening. We like coming out in Itaewon because it's a lot of fun here!

He had explained away in his Korean-English, spoken less effectively than Min-Jae whom continued to put out a feeler.

So, have you been to South Korea before? She asked.

It struck me, they were just as curious in me as I was in them, like two newly introduced cats attempting to make sense of the other. My curiosity in their country had taken them back.

Why was it I had chosen to visit? Was I going to other parts of the country? Was I going to visit the DMZ? What did I think of it?

The questions kept rolling, Min-Jae wanted to know whether or not I thought it safe to visit South Korea. Whether or not I considered visiting North Korea.

No, it's my first time here. I really like it so far. I have heard a lot of great stuff about South Korea.

Min-Jae nodded subtly.

Well, I hear you have great food and BBQ here, Your culture is fascinating and of-course K-POP!

I came off scuff faster than a shinkansen, Min-Jae chuckled hard, delicate feminine, exuberated all the while as she interlocked her arm into Tae-Song's.

Ah! This is true. Tae-Song interjected. We like to party a lot here and people like to drink a lot too. Yea I heard about that!

We continued to walk towards the four-story, off-white building, graffiti art laden on its outside, One bold in Korean calligraphy particularly stood out:

파티와 휴식의 게스트 하우□ 호□□ 장소

Colourful surf waves crashed at different tangents, its offshoot, splashed rich colour droplets reaching the far end of the building. It could be seen from the corner that led up to its main entrance.

I think this is it. This is the place.

Tae-Song blurted, in a deep stare into his smartphone. Min-Jae and I watched on. The TULLY was back in my hands. I thanked him proficiently.

Oh, it's no problem at all. It's ok. Have a great time in Seoul." He said.

I thought nothing of meeting them again. After all, this was a big city and I was to stay only a short while. They waved me on and were on their way, back down the steep alley that had led us up to the Guest House.

The archway led to the entrance was positioned through a set of gates and then a courtyard, welcomed by a great myriad of Ginkgo trees disorderly stemmed, a Barnestowne picnic bench with littered empty beer cans, danced about its narrow grooves, some beer still dripped from their brims. They could not have been abandoned long but no one was sat there. The plaque that read "Reception" was just ahead of me, lit with a small electric lamp.

—

The artist had incorporated his art around the fixtures and installations. Water and electric meters little droids. Robotic arms extruded from the upper part, its upper torso and limbs from the bottom.

A small bookshelf sat to the left of the room loaded with books. A guest was tucked into one on "being happy." I could just about make out it's cover. Another guest nonchalantly flipped through pages ''....althy eating" must be on health. He munched on a pot of noodles.

Ms. Lakatos had recommended the guesthouse, a fun home away from home as she had put it as she sat in seat K19, twizzed gently at her woven hair in braids.

She went on. I arrived pretty late that night. I was certain they had closed their doors for the night, so I rang up. The owner drove out from the hills to open up for me. This must have been around mid night. He asked if I would like something to eat and offered to cook me something before I went of to bed. I tell you, you feel very welcomed the moment you step in. She said. It's not so dissimilar to Hungarian hospitality.

Other solo travellers sat around a dinner table, well absorbed into a natter. Whatever thing they talked about, it got them really inculcated.

A worn-out couch was positioned at the far end of the room close to the stairs, another two romantics in gesture, those stairs lead to the bedrooms.

An armchair christened a corner near the breakfast area. It's occupant was a young female chatting away on her phone, watching with dotted eyes.

At the far right of the room was an even bigger lounge area. This was easy to see from the front desk. A young lady walked towards me with a smile that said "welcome" but not the sort that hinted she could be of any help. I garnered she must have also been another guest who stayed the night.

The other side of the room had guests tucked away on laptops. A good chat of old tales of travel. I only had two nights there could have stayed longer. One guest uttered from the small company.

 A sudden head appeared from underneath the counter, It seemed either to be sorting something from underneath or having a quick snack, as he chewed away with his mouth half full.

Yea sure, I would like to check in. Here are my booking reservations. In response to his inquiry.

The printed itinerary at Nari's post started to show some strain from the rain. It had been a good hour from Incheon Airport's arrival. Its' chaotic flood of passengers departed the terminal, Kamsamida! A word just learnt and soon thought to be forgotten. It all came rushing back to me.

He whizzed through the itinerary, it looked just as exhausted as I felt, ruffled to a crisp, ink strayed to the side of it.

Ray Decosta! He uttered. Yep, I have you here. You will be staying with us for 4 nights! He rambled on.

Yes, this is correct! He seemed shocked at my abrupt delivery, just as sharp as he jabbed his.

Cool!

First I need to have some form of identification and then I'll book you in. A passport will do just fine.

The scanner swizzed away and soon enough an A4 print of my mug could be seen, tucked away in his folder, bound for the office shelf. Here was a man with a face that has seen many moons go by. He worn a harness around his waist like that of a handy man equipped with small tools.

I will give you a quick tour of the place, You will be staying in room E42, it's on the second floor.

Right! Cool. He stared at me unsure how to take my response.

Here is our breakfast room. He was sharp with it.

You are welcome to help yourself to any of the free cereals and fruits we put out every morning.

Just one rule! He took a voyeur of the breakfast room.

When you use it, you wash it!

Simple rule to follow! He said.

Everyone has to do this! It keeps the place nice and clean.

There were numerous pictures of past guest plastered against a wall on the entrance to the communal. Hyun-Woo was seen holding a stiff smile in most with the exception of one, his perfectly formed teeth on display for all to see, it was centred left easy where the eye could meet it. These guest were middle aged and he seemed comfortable in their midst.

No wrinkles but strides of grey. A muscular tone to which he carried broadly, self-assuredly asserted himself. He dragged the TULLY on its hind wheels and walked broad-chested ahead.

We passed a roll of in-house greenery and he stopped to pick at a hanging pot plant. There were several more at different heights hanging ahead of us. He pulled out the roots of some dead and placed them quickly into a small bag and walked on, am a few step behind him, following obediently.

Up a flight of stairs and then another, I am too tired to comprehend a competition at this point.

 That much to carry for a 4 day stay? He asked.

The flight of narrow stairs struggled to accommodate both the case and Hyun-Woo. It's side dragged against the malt coloured wall.

It's four days here, then I am off to another country!

—

It must have been a relief for him as we reached the alphanumeric E41 written in great big zapfino fonts. Hyun-Woo flashed the key card on the electronic lock and it buzzed open E42.

You will be on the top bonk. Bed 2 over there!

He uttered, this room sleeps four people! even more sharp and to the point with it.

A small room with little to no storage space, the floor covered with piles of clothing, bonk railings were subjected to the same fate.

That dingy pool house south of Manchester came back to me. Those dimly lit lamps overseen, green surfaces of scattered pool tables dotted around the room. The fruit machine no one ever tallied to win not even Jason, that strong smell of smoked cigarette that lingered up in the air. The cheap booze no one ever drank. Yes, this dump of room reminded me of it.

The Guest House Hostel had a very well laid out website with the usual information for any guest and at this point, I questioned its authenticity.

Brilliantly taken pictures of its narrow stairways, landing, large dining area and kitchen with perspective views of the city from an arched window. An accurate depiction of its lounge with many guests sat around engulfed in some activity or another not so dissimilar from the foyer we had just walked through.

It showcased immaculately clean and organized rooms and communal and had a 4.5 on average ratings. Two of the three websites had it as a *must-stay,* but there was a disparity with this one room.

Maybe this room was a one-off, I thought.

 Hmmm! So is this room always going to be like this? I asked.

Usually it gets sorted when the owner comes back. I know the guy whose stuff this is. I will have a word with him when he gets back. Hyun-woo replied.

Any other male rooms available, Hyun-woo? Preferably one close to the windows?

Sure, there is one male room left but it's slightly bigger than this one. Cost a bit more but I will give it to you for the same price." "I am sure you will like it". "I can show it to you and you can decide. He said.

We headed out of E42 leaving the Kev backpack and the TULLY behind. Walked along a short stretch of corridor and up the next flight of stairs, lit with small xenon lights, installed into the ground as such they served as guiding lights up its path.

Buildings tend to be compact here in Seoul?' I asked.

An observation since made just being in only one building although its architecture and size were of a similar construct to its neighbouring ones.

54

We have different sizes, traditionally they can be this narrow here in Seoul. Originally this would have been two building but I got it renovated to make it one big one. He said.

We walked past room E56 and came to a stop at E57, Hyun-woo buzzed the master key card, this time and pushed the door open.

This room sleeps four too but just the three of you here for now.

Slumped on one of the four bunk was a guy. He awakened from his sleep. Perhaps he overheard Hyun-Woo's voice as we walked in, Our chatter had interrupted him.

Sorry, buddy! We woke you up! Hyun-Woo uttered.

Sorry! I joined in.

Our victim tried to return to his drowsy state, tossed and turned his duvet, over and over in a bid to get as comfortable as possible, re-enact whatever dream-state he was in before we so unknowingly interrupted. After a second or two he gave up!

Hey! That's fine. I needed it. Anton responded.

Crazy night last night? Hyun-Woo interjected. Yea dude crazy night! he responded to Hyun-Woo.

Must have slept for a good few, well over the usual eight, his body, well exhausted rest state and started to get overly uncomfortable with the idea of sleep as he rolled around in his bonk, pulled over his duvet, adjusted the cover to his upper torso.

That bunk next to the window is free. You can have it if you want Hyun-Woo suggested. .

A four-bunk-bed, one of its occupants seemed pretty easy going from sleep state, the other must have been well organized. He wasn't present, his belongings spoke volumes, shoes neatly placed underneath the bunk with two coats hanger that held its duties proudly on a hook.

Another suitcase was placed to the side, close to the other bunk. Anton either just arrived or wasn't planning on staying longer than a day. A small badge he had on his coats, a country crest.

This room is a lot better for me. I uttered.

It was a bit larger as mentioned but only had one large window that overlooked the cityscape of Seoul's hilly province.

Speed Date No 1.

Oh gosh we only have four minutes! She said. We have to make the most of it then. She said.

Hmmm! Okay, I have an idea. I said.

What is it? She asked.

 Ok you are going to tell me the weather! I mean broadcast the weather today for me. I said.

What do you mean? I don't know what the weather was like today, I hardly saw it. She mentioned.

Okay I have an even better idea.

Quickly now cause we only have 4 minutes! Well, less than four now. She chuckled hard.

Okay here is what I want you to do. Forecast today's weather for me today as weather forecasters would, only this time, you are going to tell me about your experience of this speed-dating event like a forecaster would the weather!

Okay go! I said.

Oh I don't know what to say. She said.

You now have less than two minutes left, not much to forecast on. Now go! I said.

Ok, ok I have got it, I present to you like the weather? Hmmm well…. today we have had a number of interesting looking characters! She chuckles hard.

Well some of them have been quite good but a lot have been pretty rubbish.''

Okay carry on. I urged her.

Focusing on their approach, I see a lot of lack of social skills. She said.

I am impressed! I said and she chuckled hard again.

Well am glad you like my attempt. She said.

Ok! There has been a short circuit wave of excellence in the last minute! She went on.

Oh very good! You are quite good at this. I said and she chuckled hard again.

Well thank you! Can I carry on? You are interrupting my weather presenting. She asked.

Oh am I? Sorry, carry on. I responded

Yes as I was saying there has been a short wave of excellence which has changed the outlook on things so it would seem things are on the rise. She said

This got me bolting with laughter. We both burst out with it.

Hahahaha-haha haha- haha!

Okay guys time to swap and change! The organizer announced on the microphone with a gravelling baritone.

Oh now we ran out of time. But that was fun right? I asked.

Yes it was. No one has ever asked me to present the weather before. She said.

Well that's because you look like a news presenter to me, an anchor! I responded.

Oh thanks, I'll take that as a compliment. She said.

You should. I said.

Her smile, she dazzled as she stared directly at me, those bright sparkly. For the first time that evening, I am lost for words. Not so much of the usual butterflies, predominantly related to such feelings but a feeling of refreshment, free at mind, creatively flowing. Not once did I stop and think of what next to say or how I would say it to her. Our conversations just flowed both ways, as easy as snowflakes melted away on a warm winter morning the day after a heavy snow.

So, here we are the first date. She turned up a tad late, say by a minute or so, but that was okay. The wait had been well worth it. Soon I am reminded of just how passionate at heart she is. Something about her Mediterranean glow, her essence, the warmth, the cosiness just encapsulated, am into her and she is into me. No ambiguities. Not a single shred of doubt, cluttering the cold frost of air we breathe in. Soon, her scatty rush into the room was all forgotten.

Shall we get a coffee? She asked.

Strong and heavily caffeinated, sipped as slow as possible in order not to burn my tongue and she does the same too. She mirrored me exactly. The way that I blew at the top layer to cool it and quickly took a sip soon after, she copied this exactly.

Like a metronome with a count, her white-laced converse swung back and forth. Casually she played with the tip of her hair and would quickly let it go as soon as she realized I had been watching her do it. She spoke mostly about work and it didn't bother me the least that she did. With most of her daily hours spent at the place, it made perfect sense she spoke a lot about it.

Occasionally she would catch herself getting too immersed in her own world that she would quickly throw a question at me.

Enough about me. What about you? She asked.

 What about me? I asked in response.

I mean what do you do? I mean I know what you do for work but how do you spend your day? She asked.

Clever enough not to bore her, I realized this was merely a way for her to avoid coming off too self-absorbed. She is cautious of it and subjectively passive to it. It's quite normal to want to talk about one's self. Best topic in the world.

Travelling excited me. I love to travel whenever I can. I said.

That's great, I love to travel too. So where have you been lately? She asked.

Past memories of my trip to Morocco, its intensity and getting lost within a complex network of tall mud walls intricately channelled throughout the Medina. Only to be picked up by our host at a dead-end, evading the local touts and skims. I kept my tale as light as possible.

Yes, I really like Marrakesh too. She remarked.

The tease of the night, dinner was brilliant, our second date. She has me standing in front of her door as she blew a kiss goodnight.

I'll see you around? She said.

Sure! I replied.

I blew a kiss back at her as she closes her door to the front. The intensity had been the same as the first time we met, almost like one day had merged into another and time hadn't passed at all. It was just like one single streamed day and I am lucky to have spent the evening with her again.

Our third evening together, her tenderness when she kissed, for the first time, am connected with her on a more intimate level than before. I am present at that moment and she is too. Out in the cold, sitting on a stone fence to a terrace.

I don't usually bring guys back to mine. She said.

The late night had taken a massive toll on me. I am out of juice and she is equally out too. This is good. It seemed we both needed it. She laid fast asleep, at peace with it all. I drank from a bottled water placed at the side of her bed. It is a quarter full, mostly depleted over the night's thrust.

A week goes by. Her work is taking up most of her time. I am equally pursuing mine, the allure of daily grind. We meet once, but it's only for her to offload. The strain, her life is getting the better of her and it's biting at me. Am certain she is overwhelmed by it all not going into details.

I am a listener yet again. I'd rather be elsewhere and she picked up on this.
We drifted in and out of each other's lives some more with not so much than a text that comes in so randomly it might not have been sent at all. I am listening…

—

Hey how are you doing? I just woke up from a late night shift. She said.

It's bland. I am sensing its vacancy. We drifted in and out some more, almost nonchalantly. She picked this up again.

You're not listening to me. You don't pay attention to what's important to me."

Once again I am back to zero, with no love, she was gone as quick as the buzz that had connected us.

Chapter 5

Human Connection:

19:36 pm Itaewon Seoul barbecue; Hyun- Woo had
suggested he be our guide for the night. It was our
first night in Seoul, so he suggested we head for
some famous Korean style BBQ. His choice was a
little-known place, although famous with the locals,
with authentic style of grill with charcoal.

As we walked out the infamous graffiti laden
building, Hyun-Woo looked in low spirit and I can't
exactly picture a reason why, the same brown
envelope was quickly tucked away underneath his
coat as we made our exit.

That sweet taste, strong kick of alcohol hits hard,
tasted its identifiable citrusy blend base. This had
been my first drink in weeks, my only so far.

Another sip of the shot like serving and I was settled
into my first Soju. Anton knocked them back faster
than I could. The same barge from his case, worn on
his lapel. It was blue with a mustard yellow cross, a
country crest.

I am from Gothenburg. This is kind of like *Brannvin*,
you know? Anton asked.

No not really! Hyun-Woo responded.

My roommate, the Swede, was another exchange
student embarked on a yearlong study just like the
others. *International business!* He reminded me of Pat,
the German student at the airport hours earlier.

Unlike Patrick, the Swede seemed much more
gregarious, sleeves to his well pressed, rolled up.
Worn with hem's flying loss, a country crest rested
on his chest with pride, a patriot just like Hyun-Woo.

Charmed leather ornately adorned his wrist. Time
flew as he went at his long blonde to get it out the
way, my ebony dark against his golden ivory.

More Soju was soon dancing about the linings of our
empty stomachs. Mine had a fight with the sharp
citrusy taste as it made a massive impact. Soon, the
hiss and pop could be overheard from the kitchen,
and not long after, a charcoal grill was placed in front
of us.

More servings of mint leaves and Kimchi followed,
an array of meat from an assortment of pork and beef
spat as they were placed on the grill.

I saw the face of a man many miles away in thought
Hyun-Woo's, Manager, Hostelier, Handy man and
whatever else needed doing as were welcomed to his
favourite Korean gogi-gui. The grill hissed some
more with every meat placement, storms of smoke
and steam billowed from the charcoal, our faces
engulfed in it all and the appeal for food never felt so
intoxicating.

A maid from the kitchen emerged with some eggs. As quickly as they were cracked they were done, cooked away in the fatty grease of meat that collected on the grill's peripheral. With wooden bamboo chopsticks, the meat's seasoning being quickly realized, we were thoroughly blown away. Its taste heightened by the strong kick from the Soju and hunger.

Anton was doing just as well, the same with his chopstick as proficiently as I did, you would have thought we both engaged in a crash culture course in Korean culinary.

A wide cracked smile that covered the majority of his face, it emanated cutting through the thick smoke and I got it.

I'd rather be here right now than anywhere else in the world, a refreshingly, human bond. I blurted.

Hyun-Woo placed more on the grill and proceeded to explain how to properly consume it with the use of mint leaves, an addition of spiced condiments, the meat wrapped around with another mint leaf, this added another layer of complexity. We munched away watching the sun go down. If we were in any doubt, this was food heaven and we had arrived. That brown envelope was back in Hyun-Woo's hands. He read through the paper with text drafted three quarter's down, not many on it, it looked like a sort of notice.

We surveyed Gyeongnidan Street, a very bustling street with lots of other tourists. It was the same street I had wandered aimlessly on earlier.

We headed towards Bogwang-ro and found a small bar. Hyun-Woo walked in and greeted the bartender in Korean.

Annyeong-haseyo!

We were seated and soon settling into another round of Soju, although Hyun-Woo had opted for local beer.

So how do you find Itaewon? He asked.

We had both been his guests for the night and he wanted to make sure we were having the best of times.

It's absolutely brilliant! I like it here. I blurted.

The orange Soju had taken full effect. Anton offered his perception on the place and that sombre face lifted with a cheer, the same one seen in those pictures that adjourned the wall to the foyer, stilly, it looked fresh as he had worn it genuinely.

I managed to find out my school is located close to Hungdae district. I suppose there would be a good find for me in this area? He asked.

Ideally, you can find accommodation around this same area, a small condo of sort. Said Hyun-woo.

That would be exactly my choice. I don't suppose you know how much these are likely to cost? Anton asked.

Self-contained with its own small kitchenette, if you are lucky, also at good prices! But they are rare and tend to go quickly! Hyun- woo replied.

He looked Anton in the eye as though he weighed him up against the task. Whether or not he had it in him to bag one of these rare finds.

We consumed more Soju with a raised sense of appreciation that graced our faces delicately as we doe eyed each other up, thoroughly filled from the feast.

Aniko sprung to mind, it had been a while since we parted ways at Incheon Airport. I wondered how she had faired getting to Busan.

There I was sat, thousands of miles in a new continent thinking of a girl I had only just met 18 hours ago, a new country with two stranger connecting over food and drinks with the most joyous of feelings, one of strong sentiment this human connection.

Those lime green bottles gathered into a cluster as we sat, all their content dissipated.

Enjoy yourselves!!! Hyun-Woo asserted and left with a jaunty expression, which he carried well. In his hand the same brown envelope from the reception.

The last few drizzle, we split between two shot glasses and decided on another. That prominence of Korean pop awaited us as we drowned in its beloved brew. Two westerners knee deep in it's sub culture and we had only managed to do it in just a few trying hours.

The night felt somewhat sublime than Korean. 22:35pm downtown Itaewon, humidity at high carat, heat that burnt hole in our souls, neon lights as bright as the stars would let them, it made them envy, the thundering sounds of Korean Pop, it sheared through the basement's concrete, easily we could have mistaken the place for a murky European hotspot but this was Itaewon Seoul's own nebulous district.

Anton was much better at handling the Dutch, a Swede well mannered as he spoke, our new acquaintances, two Koreans about our age, at the tavern one had taken a liken to Anton, she peered over.

Where are you guys from? Aruem asked.

We were all soon getting much more acquainted with our newly found blend of distilled beverage.

Chapter 6

The Randoms:

11:33 pm Budapest Hungarian Ruined bar 2014: Now
there stands the girl I find most attractive in the
world. Clearly a delusional mind patter but I
entertain it. But what do I say to her? What perfect
excuse to initiate a conversation? Nothing! I pounce
and ponder, ruminating at the feral bottom of my
mind. What shall I say? I could regurgitate old
conversations of past Maybe she overheard our
chatter Talks about women's inhibition. These
ponderings were happening microseconds of
walking past her in the hallway.

She had been standing a few meters from us. There
was one other female in her group of friends. Our
conversation had escalated into a debate.

Could a woman actually have a keen interest in a
guy and put out the first night? Would she feel
obliged to put out? I thought again.

They were two women in our group of six. Both took
a similar although slightly different take on the
subject. One was opinionated, which drew attention,
with ever-elevated laughter that stormed every time
she got her point across. The other supportively gave
her pennies worth in less than subdued manner.

We were initially the only ones in the far right corner of a makeshift living room, one of many ruined style rooms at the bar. This one had tons of black and white TVs and an open bar area to it.

One had a tropical theme with real-life palm tree planted indoors, a water stream and rocky boulders, it's hippie clientele sat around it. Another had a bath theme with cut in half installations. A TV screened re-runs of American 80's comedy on loop.

That large foyer with the welcome arch ''H.A.Y.M.A.R.K.E.T'' carnival crowds jeered at the music that pumped, we naturally felt we had the barn to ourselves.

Movie stars were not immune from our debate. In fact, they played the centre stage with the occasional reference to a famed star's failed marriage.

She comes across as a total head-case. I am not sure I could cope with that. One of the guys commented.

Well, I guess I sort of see what you mean, Carlos asserted.

A dragon queen! Luca added.

I doubt you get a word in, if ever had a disparity. Matthew commented.

Oh and she would totally dominate too! Luca added.

You guys talk as if you could actually get her.

She is out of your league! Fiona combated. A women is allowed to take charge and be in charge, you know! She added.

Okay, that's not what we are saying here. Luca jumped in.

We are speaking hypothetically, as if our parallels were equal, all status aside. He added.

Yea! I'll still do her! Carlos interjected. Now this is what I mean! It's plain misogynist of you to just say that. She asserted.

Six heads clambered around a barn straw table, adulated over jugs of Hungarian beer, in a yellow puffer was Matthew, whom constantly groomed at his beard, its length no longer than a few meters, at 36 he did taken a deposition of a man well in his mid forties.

Carlos worked as a chef at Coccino's, an old Italian that served the same menu since 1958. With much ardour he spoke and it was quite natural for him Most would agree men from where he came from usually did so well.

The crowd drew into fiery Fiona, the youngest of the group at 22, a year junior to Luca and Laura. It was hard to place where her heritage was from, you did regard her as of mixed decent.

All six beer jugs were consumed to the point when we saw their bottom faster than we had lifted them up. Luca went at his with a pace second to Matthew's. It is quite good sport to get through as many of these being in the military. Matthew mentioned.

When I am off shift, and usually before we all head off home, a few of us would gather at the back entrance, you know where the deliveries usually come in? We would gather a few and just knock them back before we clock out. Luca added.

Nothing beats a good beer I say! Luca interjected.

Most of the lads can hold their own, although it does tend to get a bit out of hand. You know what I mean?

Ahhh I see! Carlos commented.

Using a drink to get through the trauma, that sort of thing. Matthew added.

There was a sudden surge of silence within the group. Developed at an instant, dynamics had shifted away from frivolous to forlorn. A gloom cast upon all six of our faces as we tentatively listened.

You seem to know a lot about these things. Carlos quizzed him.

Well it is part of my job really, I work closely with soldiers returning back from the front line. I hold examinations to make sure they are fit. Psychologically fit!

So you are like a doctor? Carlos quizzed.

A psychiatric! Luca added.

A military doctor more like as I deal with all sorts, from the mundane to really serious stuff. Matthew went on.

So this will be like the PTSD sort of stuff we hear a lot about on TV. I added.

Yes, precisely so, Ray! It is one of my biggest areas of expertise. Some of these guys are just bat shit crazy! Matthew went on.

Well, l I tell you, your job is a far cry from the sort I deal with on a regular basis. added Luca. More of the same sort of madness with our guest, worst of them I did rather forget.

Summer of '12, that's when it all changed for me. Matthew commented.

Bat shit crazy, some these guys have really got it bad. he went on.
I mean I would rather forget too, but I just don't have that luxury.

That beard struck returned, he rubbed at the outgrowth of new hair that sprung from his young cheeks, even more furiously as if to relief from whatever experiences he had suddenly summoned from old memories.

A psychiatric doctor! I'm sure that must be hard work. David quizzed.

Well, it can be, but for me, I have my ways of coping with it. Things I do to get my mind off work. He responded.

Not a single word as we sat around the straw barn table with beers to nurse, every eye on every pulse cautious not to offend. We were all relative strangers moments before, randoms if you like and that floated around like butterflies on a farm. You watched and admired, careful not to trample surrounded by their gracious delicateness as they flapped about with beautiful wings.

How about you Fiona, how do you find your work? Matthew asked, breaking from the dreaded silence.

Nothing as serious as yours. She chuckled. More of the same office type scenarios, She responded.

Boardroom meetings with execs! She alerted.

Sounds interesting! And how long have you done that for? He asked.

I know it sounds fun! It's more of the usual coop settings. I am usually one or one of two women at these meetings. She went on. I joined the firm just before my twenty sixth, four Guy Fawkes's would have gone by as I remember each well, our office tends to puts on a good bonfire. She added.

We, tucked away in a Hungarian ruined bar, it's barn styled room our refuge, the beers for comfort. We had our variances as people, for being there at that particular time on that particular day, six strangers holding a discuss connecting over our differences I listened in silence for most of it, my mind wondered away like fairy flies to a flattering light bulb, still on her. The way that she walked along that narrow hallway, her shoulders adjusted so that she would just brush pass only slightly, it must have been done intentionally, I thought to myself.

I thought about my demons and hoped I would keep them away, hoped they would never poked their silly heads, at least not for the next few of hours whilst she was still stood by and the possibility was haven.

I was certain they did been listening in. Fiona's loud cries drew in for an audience even if she hadn't intended too it was the way that she was.

So what sort of guys do you date? The group fell silent, every eye on Fiona as though she had a spotlight on and was ready to perform.

Sat next to her was Laura an online marketer from the city it's quite a personal question to ask her isn't it? She interjected. Well, not really, it is only an open question to ask. I am quite curious that's all. Matthew responded.

I think you like a guy to be macho, but you also like to be in charge. Carlos added.

Well, I think most women want that. Don't they? Fiona steadily gazed in Carlos direction Actually, why can't a woman be in charge when in a relationship? She went on.

Women's rights, I say. It's the modern world after all; Matthew interjected, which garnered a few nods from the group.

Well, to be frank, it wasn't what I meant to say at all, maybe my English is a little off! I meant to say she looked the type to go for really macho guys, you know the type that spends time at the gym? Carlos added.

I see what you mean but that's a hard one to call Carlos, commented Matthew.

You all should leave Fiona alone! Laura took to defend her new and only female companion in the group.

What sort of guys do you like Laura? Matthew enquired.

The more the discussion was put on the more subdued she became, we had to agree she wasn't the type to bathe in the glory of the spotlight the way that Fiona had wanted to, a bohemian free-spirit with an acumen that quickly sent a sage grinning with envy. Earthy a scent she wore like a son of soil, her hair as bed ridden as the day it was nested. No citrus or sweet smell on her.

Her eyes glued and settled on the MOD, certain when two liked each other there is no disguise to an underline interest, although most had been oblivious to this especially Luca who had initiated strongly from the counter with six fresh Hungarian beers that steered us right in the face for a challenge.

She had liked him too. Matthew had been a lot more assertive. Laidback Luca was letting her do all the work.

All had made the trip to Budapest for the weekend. One particularly due to a longer weekend, an extra day or two made it worthwhile an escape from the mundane grey clouds of the city.

All of us total strangers bonding over cold jugs of beer, none sure what would become of these unlikely acquaintances, going with the flow of uncertainty. Maybe a lifelong friendship, maybe courtship or worst of, maybe we were all passing ships in the dead of the night conversed over these dense Hungarian jugs.

Luca earlier at the check-in desk, he is rustic in appearance, his facial hair un-kept as he carried with three twisted tongs that hanged from the bottom, a rucksack that spoke volumes of a man used to life being on the road, sure he did pick odd jobs here and there but none that needed him to be committed nor was he prepared to either. I garnered the feeling of a man running away from something.

We all were running away from something or running towards something. Fiona the youngest, the firecracker of the group, she needed her fair due too. How was it that she needed so much reassurance? Blessed with the radiance of a goddess. Laura held her earthiness down to a fine pin, a sharp contrast from her newly found acquaintance. I suppose opposites do attract.

They shared a familiar interest in the ornate, an archaeology gem dazzled around Laura's neck which she marvelled at, it's colours glowed as it hit the little light the barn room offered in the dark.

It's my grandma's old stone necklace, the one she got from grandpa, she said.

She wore it round the Analakely every Sunday. It was her favourite! she said.

Those are beautiful gems you have there.'' Luca added. The mute of the group, I just watched and nodded, my mind still on the girl from the hallway. The one I deemed the most attractive in the world, she is oblivious to me I thought, oblivious to my projections.

Analakely, that's a beautiful marketplace. Matthew commented.

Do you know it? Laura asked. It is in Africa's Madagascar right? Matthew responded.

Her smile subtly flashed at him and only he caught it with exception of the silent observer, myself a fly stuck in a sticky ointment struggling to getaway.

Randomly, Matthew had walked over and introduced himself to us at the bar, we soon established that we had all taken the same trip to escape the greys of the English clouds for much more warmer climate. The same hostel coincidentally was our refuge. My guess was that we all had chosen it due to its close proximity to the city's best ruin bars, one of which hosted us as we sat with six jugs of its favourite beer.

Every single one of us was running way from something or towards something, a need perhaps, a troubled life left behind we all needed a break as I sat silent, the quiet observer with drifted sub-consciousness my mind on the one most attractive in the world.

Our shoulders literally brushed sides and she took a slight turn to the right in my direction, she prevented further impact but also took a closer look. Our eyes met and with a slight smile she gave her approval. As much as I garnered, she had liked what she saw. I smiled back like a pro, although utterly clueless about what to do next.

A few minutes later our eyes met again, this time she was in the foyer with the other girl and am still with the five nursing down these cold brew over conversation as trivial as the day the British invaded San Juan over a dead pig.

Best thing to do is just walk over to her and get a conversation going.

That thought sprung up and I ran with like good piece of wisdom uttered by a wise old man.

I found myself standing in front of her. Although I was unsure as to what pace got me there, I was glad I made the call. She was seated alone, her legs jolted as she sifted through her phone.

Hi, How are you doing there? My opener and I hoped it did do the trick.

That brief moment passed, it felt like an hour had gone by. "Just fine!" She responded.

She broke a smile from her previously bound lips.

And how are you doing? She asked.

Her tall, slender frame moved in utter symphony as she leaned forward in the cold breeze of the night and I felt it.

Damn!

Another thought that sprung to mind. This was mid-March in Budapest with lows of 12C and on my back was a thinned fabric shirt, the thought of it complemented well with in the temperate of Hungarian spring I hadn't taken the evenings chills into consideration.

Was it the element of the moment that had heightened my senses or the sudden chills of the evening spring? I could hardly tell.

She appeared similarly nervous too. Although doing a brilliant job of concealing it.

I am doing okay, I responded back.

Her bronze-like skin tone, angular features lean in muscles, a Presbyterian disposition.

Do you ever wonder why the stars twinkle?

Saying whatever came to mind first might have been a weakness by admission, but it was an effort nonetheless.

Ohh that's nice, I am not sure why they do. Do you? Do you mind if I sit down"

And immediately this felt too awkward. Almost jump-gun like.

Sure! The familiar silence rolled in again.

Back at the group, the discussion had drifted to politics. Matthew had done well to break Laura from it. Both were on a sofa in the bath themed room.

The venue bustled with people. The music was loud and vibrant. Some pop on rotation, the cut with each verb that oscillated with an electronic swish!

''Dance! Dance! Slow down I wanna slow down''.
Boomed from the speaker adjacent.

Every twenty-five seconds on the rpm it came on repeat, the time about one in the morning. Progressively she leaned out, my attempt to learn more about Maria below.

So where are you from?

 She smiled, almost indicative of knowing our brief encounter was going nowhere, likely to come to a prompt end sooner rather than later. Her voice progressively deepened as if sudden surge of testosterone had been dowsed as she sipped on her drink.

Fiona's voice suddenly peaked in from behind.

Do you know where Laura is?

She placed her hand firmly on my left shoulder.

I have her bag here and will be heading back soon. She said.

Hmm! I think she is somewhere with Matthew. I said. You're staying at the same place as us aren't you? She asked.

Yea, The Garden Valley.

Fiona's arm perched on my shoulder, she held it there longer than usual enough for me to see the veil lifted from Maria's raw-boned face, her interruption had ushered in a sudden paradigm.

Hey sorry, I am Fiona what's your name? She asked.

Sorry I should have introduced myself. I am Maria.

And I don't know your name by the way nor do I know yours. She referred to me.

Well, I should have told you!

It's Ray.

Maria, at 5 feet 10 inches, was she also running away from something or towards something like we all were?

She had the looks from untrained eyes perspectives, the build of oblong outgrowth. Fiona left us drenched with a freshness of new hope. It was just like in the hallway only this time I knew her name. ''Maria!'' She is not a stranger now.

Modelling gigs rarely revolve around just looks and build you know. She said.

There is much more they tend to look for, these designers. She went on.
As gravely as she could, she went about the conversation as if a familiar old ghost had suddenly reared its head.

They have their pick. Lots of girls dream of doing this, all too willing, most of them, young, aspiring and eager to please. She went on.

I fell into Journalism instead.

One she shared with a childhood friend. Long gone were her leg strut dreams. In came an ebullient drive for Journalism. But for now, she was more focused on seeing Europe.

Sao Paulo, Brazil is my hometown. Buenos Aires is a great city.'' She commented as we went about the map of Central and South America.

She remembered her old minder, the one that danced the tango late into the night in La Boca. She made a dozen or so trips to New York and two or so trips to Paris. The south of Spain had been on her bucket list, but she couldn't quite garner a reason to go there.

I reckoned these were the days she had attempted to procure her modelling career. We almost spoke until the crows made their morning croak.

Maria by my left, her hand snuggly warmed mine as we headed towards the crowded dance floor. A great big pine woven archway that spelt out the words; *T.H.E V.I.N.E.Y.A.R.D* hovered above on entry.

Credits given where due Hungarians certainly mastered the art of imagination. The Vineyard a place supposedly represented ripe with possibilities for the picking and with the right aptitude, one could assert and be rewarded with riches of finely fermented hedonistic conquest.

The music played, some Latina, her vocals subtle as she sang. The thought that she could be a natural at this had crossed my mind the moment the music changed and the Latina went about her serenade. Almost instinctively she moved in a lateral undulation, in symphony with the music. Her hips swung from side to side. Her eyes fixated on mine, as would a predator on its prey and the sudden realization. Only a minute ago she was going to pie me off. Now, in somewhat perfect unison, it seemed no one existed in the evidently crowded vineyard.

The bestial crowd pushed, they shoved and that got a bit too much, whatever personal space we established was soon long gone! She was in my arms and hers were around my neck.

Sunday mornings are typically to have an air of incompleteness to them, the want, the long for more of the same of Saturday. A sudden realization of come-down. Usually, the next 24 hours never felt so saddening, but this one had been different. There was a beautiful woman lying next to me. We had sex all night and although we were exhausted, it was exhilarating. We had opted to go back to her place, a much bigger private space.

I remembered the walk back being ceremonious. We constantly stopped and frolicked at every dim lit street corner. Eventually, we got back to her place. The journey should have taken 25 minutes with a straight walk through the town centre, but it took well over 45 minutes. It was fun. Up the stairs, she gave me a brief smooch and then up another before the inevitable landing. She had me and I had her.

A walk around downtown Nagykorut and the scent of coffee never felt better. Quaint bakery shops, antique and butchers shops lined the streets. We were both silent taking in the fresh morning breeze. We both needed it.

For a brisk moment, nothing else mattered. Being in her presence was all that seemed virtuous, which was a vast contrast from hours before. She held my hand firmly and let her fingers slide between mine the way she did back at the vineyard. She held tight and looked over to me, similar to what she did in the hallway.

There was a mystic to the moment. Neither of us were sure we were going to meet again. It wasn't a lingering thought, but one that had crossed my mind at early that morning.

I remembered the sip of water from a glass she had left on the counter. She had put two out the moment we stepped in, but neither of us had time to drink from them.

I remembered her pace, that of a hare's, the way she had taken off her gear.

"Aren't you going to take yours off?" She asked.
"You're just going to stand there and watch me?"
She enquired.

Immersed, I observed just how beautifully put
together she was as she stood in stack virtue.

The glass tasted funny. It had absorbed a decent
amount carbon dioxide from the air over course of
the night but this didn't matter to me much. My
thoughts were, as usual, festered on much more
cardinal schemes.

Out in the fresh morning Hungarian breeze, I
pondered how I could make those moments count?
Make them last longer than usual. Almost
immediately it dawned on me. These were the very
thoughts that had brought about my downfall with
Melanie.

We wandered some more round Nagykorut. The
scent of freshly baked bread oozed from the bakery
shop that mastered the corner. Strongly brewed
coffee was dispensed into the short espresso cups
that patron sipped even slower than breeze. She blew
a kiss from the Airport taxi rank and I remembered it
well. Not much of Budapest was seen with my next
flight to Translyvania boarding.

Chapter 7

K-Pop:

20:47 pm Itaewon South Korea Saturday: So what do you call a girl that is not dating? Han Sonyeo! But we are not Han Sonyeo sorry! That's okay. He replied.

Anton had started off on a seemingly negative note and was getting the rejections thick and quick! The queue was long and the crowd nonchalant. Not particularly in a straight line more of a cluster that snaked all the way to the front of an American style coffee dinner. The owners had long closed so no obstruction happened to the service they offered at daytime.

Areum and Hye the two at the bar earlier, Hye smoked a thinned style cigarette. Blew her exhalation away from the pack. Areum arms were crossed, intensely she steered at Anton an attempt to disarm him instead it heighten his interest.

So you think you are funny? She asked.

What do you mean? Anton responded

You said we look like geisha. She said. That's in Japan! She said.

I am sorry! He replied.

Well, have you ever seen geisha before? She asked.

They spoke in a konglish dialect particular to the southern region of Korea.

Their faces are white with red lipsticks! They don't dress like this! Areum commented.

Equally, I struggled with her apathy towards Anton, his train of thought was pure intent. Had he, in fact, been negging? It hadn't been quite a strong one if this was his intent.

The girls more western in couture. They looked like they had just finished from a cooperate gig and were out to unwind. Sure, they were pale in complexion, but not pale-faced as a geisha would be.

So, are you both from Seoul? Anton asked.

No, we are both from the same place, Daegu. Areum responded. Do you know it? She asked

No, I don't. He replied.
Oh! It's not far from Busan. Do you know Busan? Aruem asked again.

Yes, I do. I interjected it seemed we had started to loss interest.

A friend of mine is actually traveling there. I added.

For a brief moment, the thought of Aniko sprang to mind *"How was she fairing on her adventure?"* Mine seemed to be going well, at least well enough that Areum had decided we were much more fun to talk to.

The dire conversationalist Anton from Gothenburg, seemed to want to dig us an even bigger hole than the last one. *"What in the hell was his problem?"* I thought at the time.

Hye just seemed to smile, giggling the whole time. She smoked on her thinned cigarette and was careful to exhale away from the pack.

So, you said you are from England? Hye asked
Where in England? Areum asked.

I am from the North. Manchester? Do you know it? I asked.

Ohh Hmmm! Eh, do you know Park? Hye asked.

He is a footballer. Really famous here in South Korea. Aruem interjected Played for Manchester United. Hye commented.

I like him a lot. She said, which broke Hye's spell of silence as though her amniotic sac had just given way to a flood of laughter.

Dangsin-ui syupeo hogam! She commented.

Elleun nolliji mala! The two went off in their native dialect.

My cousin hmmm, she/he goes to a college there. Hye commented. Do you know it? she asked.

Sure! I replied.

Have you heard of Robin hood? I asked.

Robin ehh hood? Ehhh! Emmm. Aruem persisted for a while in a clueless bout.

He wore funny green spandex, stole from the rich, gave to the poor. I commented to help.

They both were clueless. I went on.

He lived in the forest? Used a bow and arrow as weapon? I asked, Anton seemed to take a backseat to the conversation observing what little rapport we had managed to build.

Ahhhh! Eyyyyy! Yes! Yes! Robin Hundeu Aruem commented. Yes! Robin Hundeu! Robin Hundeu! Hye joined in.
She jumped into an animated giggle. The whole evening had been spent attempting to shoehorn her into a conversation and all it took was a silly old tale of a group of bandits in green tights.

Robin Hundeu! I like hmm, old folk ehh tale.

And you are from Sweden! Hye asked. Yes! Anton replied.

How did you know that? he asked.

I can see your barge, pointing to the small country crest that sat on his right lapel. It is the flag of Sweden. She commented.

Yes you are right! I am Swedish! Have you been to Sweden before? He asked.

Ermm! No. Hye responded.

The crowd thinned ahead, the music got louder. Not too dissimilar from the music that played at the bar, Korean K-pop.

How long, are you staying for? Areum asked.

Well, I will be here for 4 days and then I plan to go off to Sapa. It's in Vietnam. It's really, beautiful there.

The beer, cold and crisp, was the same as we had earlier at the small tavern. The emptiness of thoughts, an over-familiar feeling, one of un-comfort yet an underline tingling of excitement.

I would rather be here. Here is much more better. Better than being anywhere else, loud as the music was, its jubilant young, joyous with every Korean sing along that came on.

I am far away from the mundane, the conveyer belt, the static I experienced as a social-economic blue collar. I am drenched in sweat from the heat. The humidity had gotten me. It made my muscles tense from brutality of the crowd.

Here, I supposedly felt freer, although a social construct of it's own. Areum had mourned of the long late nights, the long late company dinners. She got on well at work, that wasn't quite the issue. It was the long hours being spent in the same space, the same people day in, day out, that had gotten to her. That was what she wanted to get away from, what she inevitably wanted to run as far away from.

It had become quite exhausting, as she put it. She came up with plans of her own. Plans she could one day get away from the mundane, the routine. Plans; ones she couldn't quite muster the courage to embark on.

Inside was a venue rammed worst than a ranch, Areum walked over, in her hand a beverage, she sipped and watched the jubilant crowd. We both weren't sure if this was going anywhere. At some point we both seemed to just play, dipping the straw in and out of the ice that floated.

It gets, really rowdy here, later on. You see k-pop, in full glory, commented Areum.

We have been waiting to actually witness it in person. Commented Anton. I get the feeling she much more preferred Areum. Hye was way too reticent in disposition.

I can imagine the crowd gets really wild later on. He added.

Yes! Just you wait and see. She was lunging for Anton's chest. The alcohol kicks in and all the boys go wild. It is really liberating and fun to watch. She commented.

So, do you get wild as well? Asked Anton.

No! No! Just the boys mostly, although, I have been that way, sometimes. She added.

Sure! He added I mean a little bit of fun is good, right?

She surveyed the room, brushed her hair to the side. The look of interest projected onto him. He seemed to be doing a lot better now. He seemed to have won her over, gotten over this past bungle.

I overheard them, something about puppies and which was cuter? Shih Tzu or Pomeranian?

It's so cute! She commented.

Yes, they are a curious breed. Veryyy, playful! Yes, and friendly. I still, think the Shih Tzu is a cuter dog. Small, so cuteeee! She added.

Hye was lost and seemed to be buried in the glared screen of her phone.

"See! Lots of charisma!" She added. "They are quite spunky," Anton went on. "Yes I know, but I like that!" "The Shih Tzu for me." She smiled widely at Anton.

The beer bottle was lighter in weight as I held it to the light, it's liquid content exhausted as I drew for a drink. I looked into the eyes of my slender companions. ''She had hers all but gone. I'll enquire anyway a good excuse to make my escape.
It's busy at the venue, cluster of stern, eagerly waiting punters. I'll come to accept there is no getting past. The more they made me wait, the more sober I got, then came an unexpected tap on my left shoulder.
Hey, you The voice said.

Hey! Hmmm! Haaa! Pat right? It was Pat the German from Incheon.

Yea right! It's Ray, right?

Yea! I didn't expect to see you here. He said. Me too! I replied.

''Talk of a random encounter not going anyway.'' I thought to myself.

So, how have you found your first day? I asked.

Ahhh! So far, it has been brilliant. Seems it's all getting sorted pretty quickly. He said.

You're here to study, right? International business, right? I asked.

———

Yes, International Relations, rather.

But you remembered. He said.

Of course I did.

Who are you here with? He asked

Ohh, well I came with my hostel buddy. He's Swedish.

Ahh! Okay. He said.

Who you here with? I asked.

Some of my school colleagues, that big crowd over there. Do you see it? He asked.

They're the ones not jumping around like the others. He went on.

Hahahaha!

We heard it was a niche night, so the organizer made arrangements for us to come here. He said.

Very good!

Come say hello. He suggested.

We wiggled through the jumping crowd. Pat was in front and he moved through the crowd like a pro. He gets barged from all corners and the after current leaves me with somewhat of a lesser barrage to work through.

Hey, guys! This is Ray. We met at Incheon Airport earlier today. He was on the plane in from Beijing.

Hey! Ray? How are you? How are you doing Ray? The group asked.

The effect of alcohol had long taken effect with this group. I, on the other hand, was on a comedown in need of a refresher.

Just fine! Just fine. I said.

What's your name? I asked.

I am Mateo! He shook my hand vigorously.

I am Josh, Hi,

I am Brittany!

Eloise, Hi

I am Matt.

And with that, the group introduced themselves. It was quickly established that all six of them stayed at the dorm house organized by the school.

No, we're Canadian not Americans. Montreal in the house! Mateo was by far the loudest of the group.

I am from Finland, by the way! Eloise the sunbird — blonde, short and petite. She wore her hair short and cropped. She was reserved, quite silent at first, and said little. She did even less, but sipped on a daiquiri.

I know, Pat mentioned it. She said.

He had been eager to introduce me to all his new colleagues with whom he had become acquainted within the last hours.

 Let me take a Polaroid of you all. He said.

He had his Polaroid with him again. It seemed like he took it everywhere imaginable and took shots of whatever interested him as the sun kissed goodbye to am emerging moon. The group quickly gathered together to pose for one of Pat's Polaroids. Soon, it would make his folder. I hoped he had found a way to keep them all in there.

So, are you here on your own? She asked.

Well no! I came with a few people. I might have lost them by now. I said.

Ohhh! I hate when that happens. She said.

 It's okay they are on the other side. I am pretty sure I'll find them later. I said.

So, are you a student too? She asked.

Ohh! No, I happen to be traveling. I said.

Oh! That's cool. She said.

Eloise, whom I had thought to be the most reserved of the pack, enquired at a hare's pace.

So, where are you headed to next? She asked.

Vietnam, I hope! in response.

The venue was to capacity. The noise made it so that it was difficult to comprehend whatever it was she had intended to say. I managed to gather she had never left Finland and, like Pat, chose Seoul for similar reasons: to explore it's culture and food, as well as meet new people—locals and foreigners alike.

She had been in the country a week ahead of registration for the program. She had a good enough time getting acclimatized to its culture, language, and some of its customs. Pat returned.

Let me take a Polaroid of you two! He suggested.

He snapped away. He depressed the lever on the camera and an 8.8cm frame of Eloise and myself quickly ejected from its bottom base.

I am keeping this one for me. She said.

Eloise grabbed the newly printed Polaroid.

It's a cute photo! She said stuffing it into her handbag almost immediately.

The music was getting louder by the minute, or so it seemed. I could hardly hear a word or make out what it was she attempted to say.

"*She's struggling to make conversation.*" I thought to myself. Pat was well into the spirit of the event. He was occupied taking Polaroids of his new colleagues. I was sure he wouldn't mind me walking off with her.

Let's go out for some air. She suggested almost instinctively, maybe she read into it doe-eely. My phone vibrated and it's a message from Aniko, the lady who sat at K19 on Cathy Pacific.

I still managed remember our conversation fresh as a pitta.

Areum, Hye, and Anton were somewhere in this club. I was sure they would wonder where I was this whole time. Perhaps they thought I was still at the bar, attempting to get a drink they might have thought.

Speed Date No 2.

So okay, tell me something. If you were stuck on an island and you had to take only two items, what two things would you take?

Two things! I am allowed only two things?

Yes, just two things.

Ok, ok, hmmm! Let me see, well it will have to be an encyclopaedia! And….a big block of cheese! Cheese!!! Yes cheese!

She observed the look of bewilderment that grazed my face.

That's interesting, you clearly like cheese.

Yes I like cheese a lot.

Ok, that settles that. Encyclopaedia! What would you need that for?

Well, the encyclopaedia will be for me to read.

Yes I figured this out, it's quite obvious but why you need it to survive being on a lost the island?

Well I figure am going to be on this island a while.

Yes, this is correct.

So I can study the encyclopaedia and become really, really smart. I can survive and get myself off the damn island.

Hahaha… Clever answer!

Ok, enough of me, how about you? What two things would you take with you?
Ok I will take a knife.

Ok why a knife?

So I can kill stuff. You know for hunting and cutting things down.

Well, you know you can make a knife out of sharp objects too. She remarked.

She was being competitive, testing my strength, checking if I was firm in my choice of items or if she could persuade me to change them.

Ok, yes you can, but this will be my choice.

Ok, and your second choice?

It will be a Lighter.

A lighter! Whatever will you do with that?

Light stuff up, start a fire!

You know that there are ways of starting a fire without a lighter? Suppose you run out of lighter fluid, what will you do then?

Well, in the meantime my lighter will serve me well. I can worry about other means of starting a fire later. Besides, I would have gotten used to being on the island and possibly sourced out other means of supply by then.

Hmmm wishful thinking, you're a true optimist!

Her second test, she once again checked my strength in choice. The bell chimes and the allocated four minutes was up. Time to move on. She leaned in with her chin, slightly lifted up.

I'll see you again.

Of course, there was a big smile hidden away as I walked. I walked from table No. 7 with the biggest poker face concealed deep within. Two days go by and I am high on hopes like a gasoline filled motor engine jostling for a bolt. I sat in front of a glaring screen, opening emails, many of which of unnecessary means as none would be taken up. One from the organizer sits buried in midst of the cluster of junk mails. A quick click to open and I login. I stared at the text, never had I felt so much joy from reading.

''It's a match!''

You can imagine my excitement. I had dreamt it up and now, miraculously, it was happening. I wished well in my good fate and now it's here. I only had the one match, but one that had mattered much, out of sixteen. I hot seat-hopped; she had been the one that made a lasting impact in the short four minutes allocated to each seat hop. No consideration was being given to what should be said at this particular moment and being equally carried away, by the excitement of it all

''Its a match!''

I am tapping away at the keys of my laptop as fast as my fingers would let me, and as a capable typist, my talent took me. My first email to her, with no time to waste, read:

Subject: *''Why wait!''*

''Hello my island playmate.

Good to see we get to chat again.

Have a good Friday.

Let's arrange to meet soon.

XX.

Ray.''

To think of it what would one do, that all too familiar, radio silence returned. Once again, I am back to zero, with no love prospect to boast.

Chapter 8

Taxi Driver:

South Central Europe 14:25 pm 2014: The text came in swift and heavy if you could weigh an electronic bit, it felt like a ton. She had not been in contact for over a year, most of the communication had been one-sided. It was mostly prompted by myself. Talk of a bad infatuation. One that could have been easily avoided. Prolonged due to a massive state of disillusion.

My ego got in the way. I couldn't deal with the loss as appropriately as I previously thought.

"*Hey Ray,*

I hope you are doing okay? I just wanted to get in touch with you as I know it has been a while and things didn't particularly go well between us. It was not entirely your fault so don't blame yourself, I was to blame for some of it too. If you have some time maybe we can have a chat?"

All the best,

Melanie xx."

My first instinct was to ignore it. I had been doing just fine. It hadn't occurred to me just how much was buried deep down. Those raw emotions were the same ones that had left me crippled.

I hadn't acknowledged her existence in a while and things were starting to feel a bit lighter and brighter on the inside, which was good. I looked back at the long 8 months, the relatively happier side, and then a year and a half, desperately clinging onto make it work. I sparingly stayed in touch, not discounting the occasional insipid web stalk. Damn infatuations!

She never kept web accounts, no social media. She had always been that way, even when we met. It raised my level of crippling curiosity.

''Had she had been someone else's unicorn?'' I thought *''I am certainly not her first, the way she had expertly disappeared off my radar.''*

I had a part to play as well. I enabled an addiction, an obsession, one with a spell and nagging desperation to break free from.

"What had she been up to?" "Who was she really?" "Why so much secrecy?" "Who was her family?"

Well, she spoke little about them.

"I reckoned she had a past, one she wanted to protect."

I ignored the bright green banner that displayed her message and moved on.

The walk through old Transylvanian city of Cluj-Napoca was liberating. The feeling of being in an ancient worn down yet captivating setting gave a certain mystic and pre-eminence from the well organized.

My flight had been a short one out of Ferenc International Airport, Budapest. I am traveling with just the KEG a blue backpack. The TULLY was unnecessary. It's a short trip. I slogged the blue over my left shoulder and braced for the high altitudes. We arrived at a less subdued airport than the last one. Maria and they way we had left things open.

Most people had been passengers from Budapest, lots of French-speaking nationals in business suits. "Bine Ati Venit!"

The arrival foyer was deserted as quickly as it had been filled a few minutes earlier. We all walked past the small kiosk near the exit and I stopped for a small latte.

The Deco somewhat minimal enlarge poster to other European cities. I took it in as I sipped from the small cup, destination Rome, Prague, London, Paris, Berlin and Crete, each well briefed, an iconic representation of the city for instance, Big Ben for London, Paris The Eiffel Tower, Budapest an old Orthodox Cathedral and Rome The Citadel.

The walk around the foyer was a bit eerie. For a while it seemed extremely quiet as it was deserted as quickly as it was filled. It felt like no one left the place. No one ever travelled out.

The sign with an arrow, bright white, led straight to the departure, but no one was there. My curiosity waddled me on like a pet dog. Finally. I saw an information board with scheduled flights in and out of Napoca. There were a total of three late evening flights scheduled, not a huge amount.

It is way cheaper to travel by bus. Yes, it takes a long time but it is the best way. Iulia had mentioned.

I saw the information board with numbered destination on display. There wasn't much going out of the place. Mustard yellow text oscillated the flight information for the next departing flight.

"Yes I have been to this one, and that one, and this one" "Well, I plan to go to that one next." Muttered to myself.

Flights	Time	Gate
PARIS France A11	18:34 pm	
BUDAPEST Hungary	18:45 pm	A21
VERONA Italy	19:15 pm	A12

The caffeine fix took good measures. I am bestowed with alertness, a readiness, one to brave this whole new world. I tossed the polystyrene into the mesh basket by the exit. I walked pass the lined taxi rank, hawk stalls that made to the main road. Again, I reflected Iulia's advice.

It's the best and cheapest way to get into town. Take the local bus! She said.

On the road for the bus stop, a friendly looking Romanian man approached.

Taxi! Do you want Taxi?

What could go wrong here? If I took this man's service, I can at least enquire the cost beforehand. That would be a smart assured way of not getting ripped off.

I felt exhausted, not much sleep had been observed the night before. I put aside Iulia's advise. The late-night hangover at the ruined bar took full toll, that early hour set off time. I was half asleep the whole way to the Ferenc.

A quick taxi ride to old town seemed a good way to relax. In addition, Nicolae was bound to know the roads well. We went back and forth and agreed on a price.

19 Lei. You take me to old town, okay Yes sure, 19 Lei old town,

Come! come!

He grabbed the blue from my hands and threw it to the back of his cab. He requested I sat in the front and I thought nothing of this. He is a friendly old man, possibly in his fifties. He seemed to love a good chat and I was bup for one too. So I found myself in the front of his old Peugeot, headed for old town.

So, you've been to Romanian before? He asked whimsically.

Surely, this would lead somewhere, but where? We had agreed on a price. What schemes could he be drumming up.

I decided to engage.

No, this will be my first time in Romania.

To put him off his schemes, I tell him about Iulia, how she had warned about taxis in and around the airport. His ears stood alert. I could tell he listened with intent.

Her advise on the bus was, "It's the best way to get into old town.

We drove a good mile and a half through the hot dusty terrain. There were lots of mid-size towering buildings, some modern, some worn out, and some thoroughly dilapidated. He resumed.

This is a beautiful country, right? Yes, it is. My country is beautiful. He proclaimed.

I like it here. The weather is absolutely marvellous. I took in the hot rays that the sun served us on a platter. It was mid-march.

What do you do? He enquired, whimsically.

 Oh, do you mean back home?

Yes, yes, what you do back in your country? He asked.

Well, I work a professional job. Being careful not to disclose too much or too specific.

Very good, very good. It pays very well? Yes it is okay. I replied.

Covertly, I surveyed his cab. He had an old beaten down Peugeot. Its dashboard was just as sun bitten and worn. It smelt of engine oil, the sort of cab you pick up from a junkyard. We were now twenty-five minutes into the old town. We came upon some local traffic and I took a quick glance at the back seat. Not much was here, just some old dusty worn out seats. No seat belts either.

We get to old town soon. Nicolae insisted.

I took a quick glance at the meter and its work rate, we were 21 leis in and I thought the better of it.

We can't be far now. I asked.

The traffic moved slowly, building up with every passing minute. My taxi driver Nicolae had a better idea in mind, a detour!

A much better faster route. He says.

We took the first left, then went up a narrow residential before a right turn. We stumbled on a roadblock, which restricted access by car. He proceeded left, then another left up another equally narrow residential. All the while, it left like circles on a Russian roulette, one more roadblock and we could have had it. We would have been back in that jam. He turned right and we stopped stack in the middle of the cobbled road.

Where is this place? Where you want to go? He asked.

Well, I don't know. You are the taxi driver. You should know.

Let me see address again? He requested.

Over went the printed itinerary with the address on

''Nr 32- 34 Strada Decebal Cluj 4449034''

Okay, Okay, I know. I know. He insisted.

He swung his wheels to the right and made a U-turn. Then he took a left. We took a right turn, then another. It almost felt like going in spirals. The meter read well into the thirties. We arrived at yet another cobbled road and slowly made an entry. He parked and made a quick whimsical glance across. The meter bill read into the fifties.

It was difficult to criticize Nicolae. Was he trying to help? Did he have good intentions? Was his detour one of good gesture? I pondered.

The traffic was too bad today! He insisted. We'll still be there if we stay. You see, I get you to your hotel fast my friend. He went on.

Lei scribbled on a piece of paper, double the original 19, and handed it to me.

What is this? We agreed, 19 Lei I quizzed. My friend! My friend. You see traffic too bad today. I help you, you get here no traffic, you see. He insisted.

I took a long look at him. I ruffled deep in my jeans for change from the coffee stand. I handed him 32 lei in total and handed it over.

This is all I have. It's all you will get.

If he's having me on, then this old boy had got me. I thought.

It all seemed to be in good fate. He deserved his pay. I thought. Besides, he had the look of a man in dire need and he could do with some extra pay.

I grabbed my backpack from the back and said my goodbyes. My old friend wished me well. I am certain he was smiling as he counted his newly earned Lei. Indeed I might have been had.

"Why do we travel???

Jet Lag, sickness, stomachs ache. A general sense of confusion. Expenses, early morning red eyes flights. The possibility of eating at the worst restaurant and staying in pest infested hotel rooms.

We pack our bags mind-numbingly, always confused about what to bring. We brave airport traffic, subject ourselves to being searched, patted down, unclothed at times to be faced by hundreds of tiny tedious, yet all-important, duly decisions and all that even before leaving. Once on the plane, you're sweaty, clueless about what to do for the next hour or even the next day. Sitting, waiting and hoping patiently.

We walk for the longest time, nomadic people always on the move. We go through the worst travel conditions than what we have to date. We go to find greener pastures, new land, and other shiny opportunities. Today, most of us sit in front of our computers, hopefully doing a job we enjoy to pay the bills, with taxes at the end of the month. To continuously live the same routine at every new dawn.

I travel to search for discomfort, to be put in a situation that doesn't make sense, to push my mind to think beyond my daily routine. To learn and become a better version of myself. To realize what I have been doing wrong and how I can mimic the good I find in other cultures. And to feel small, humble and consequent. At all over the world we live in. I travel to be real, to go back to what it means to be human, to munch on life one last time!

We travel to break the norm, to attempt to regain a sense of adventure arriving in a foreign part. Exhausted yet immediately fulfilled. It is human nature to challenge monotony, to be continuously curious. There is a peek at your partner's phone or their shoulder, or perversely watching how citizens of a different country eat, interact and kiss". You-tuber, Author- Erwan Heussaff.

I looked back at her text. Melanie's jotter, its last lines…

"If you have some time maybe we can have a chat."

The weight returned. It was sudden, but not as heavy as it was before. I retreated to take a better view of the room I had arrived in. Nicolae's antics had long been behind me.

It's nice and clean, an open brick wall that gives off an earthy warm ambiance. Its deco of brown-stoned slate mosaic, a walk in wet-room adorned with a sterling head. There was a 45 degrees water pour that dissipated my entire shoulders, first with a chill that quickly warmed, then became too hot to bear. I stood motionless, lathered as the steam bellowed. The glass planed walls engulfed me.

I recounted my last moments with Maria: the sweet rose smell of her hair, her apartment overseeing the gorge, the taxi ride in to the Ferenc.

"If you experience sadness without craving that the sadness goes away. You continue to feel sadness, but you do not suffer from it. There can actually be richness in the sadness. If you experience joy without craving that the joy lingers and intensify, you continue to feel joy without losing your peace of mind."

Yuval Noah Harari.

Chapter 9

I am not a Random:

Cakeshop Itaewon 00:15 pm Sunday: The smoking area was packed with smokers, we stood there, but neither of us smoked. We stood in an area designated for lung poppers, suggestively slow stuffing ,and yet, we were quite happy to be passive participants.

It had been easier to hear there, a lot better than being on the inside of the clubhouse. I could barely hear what she had been trying to say to me the whole time. Out there, I could stand. Rest assured, we weren't being pushed or shoved in the midst of a K-pop special.

The tension had been building, mostly through body language. Hers was a curiosity clearer than an Amethyst crystal. It was evident how little experience she had in the way of covert signalling. Being more accustomed to females with an attuned sense of the art and could, with a hint decipher between the lines. She cared little about disguising hers.

I bet you do this a lot? She asked.

She leaned in even more. The summer months were nearing its end and the humid heat could be felt with optimum brilliance: The sweat, the wetness, the cling of my now, drenched dark vest. I had opted for a change as soon as I had a chance to check in at the guesthouse. The journey in from Beijing had been horrendous. My vest had been a thoughtless mistake, one that could have been easily avoided. I endured the heat right from the airport in and embraced every air-conditioned room and carriage from Incheon.

It wouldn't have taken that long to fling open the flap to my TULLY and grab a much more comfortable one. This cotton woven black simply conducted the heat like an oven.

Our nonchalant companions were casually smoking, some engaged in conversations, or doing both at the same time. The chatter was loud and mostly in Korean.

So, how do you arrive at this thought, then?

She smiled and held it for a while. She rocked her sidelines slightly as she tiptoed, almost as if to dance around the topic. That very moment was reminiscent, not just of the past, but of someone else too, so familiar, yet unfamiliar.

I pondered as she stood there, just looking at me. Where was this déjà from? It seemed like one that had come with much pain and yet joy beyond comprehension. Maria sprung to mind! That same flirtatious stare, that coy dance, and she knew more than she was letting on too.

I just know. She said.

An earlier conversation with Areum had been different as we walked the crowded streets, seemingly easy to hold, although somewhat on the surface. Now, here stands Eloise. She is projecting, thirsting for an adventure, a lust. She is making it blatantly obvious, too. It's too easy, and yet her appeal holds strong with me. She is like good Jazz that takes you unknowingly on a ride, a wave of continuous trajectory, up and up, but not too high to go beyond comprehension.

Well, I am no random! No Random! Well, what do you mean?

A young Korean chap interrupts.

laiteo iss-eoyo? He asked.

Sorry I don't speak Korean. In response.

Ahah! Lighter? Lighter? He asked.

Oh sorry, we don't smoke. In response.

Ohh! Ok! Ok! Kamsamida! And with that he was off.

Her vest hugged her slim frame enthusiastically, Her blue denim matched well with it. She could have easily fallen out of a Gap ad campaign. That good Jazz feel! Visite Du Vigile, a conversation of bodies with relatively little else to say.

"I could play this really cool what's the haste? I know very little about her. She knows nothing about me. The night is relatively young. Plus, it could be one of those meaningful connections."

There were moments with Eloise that felt refreshing. She was a stranger, a harmless one at that. She looked to me as though I were a mystic, some flower, a petal she needed to pull apart for secret nectar.

Who knows? She chuckled.

Once, a good acquaintance told me; "great things come out of a single moment of encounter, you can never be too sure what would happen." She said.

Well, you are right, I do get this a lot. I can't get them off me.

She chuckled.

Well, I think I need to be careful around you. She added.

That feeling of euphoria came upon us as we stood inches apart, a sense that you had waited your whole life for this very moment, with not a minute to waste. It was to be captured, or lost forever.

It was too much to bear, it seemed the inside crowd had been turned on its side and emptied out into the yard, our once intimate space, established was long gone.

It's getting rowdy here, we should go inside. She suggested.

Her lower jaw, her chin a 38 degrees angle I lifted and leaned in for a kiss. She didn't hesitate and this didn't surprise me. It was soft and long, warm like a scoop of cobbler.

The crowd almost as if non-existent as I protected as though a tortoise would do it's interior. I could not care less about the occasional jab from the side. She could not care less about the occasional steers.

She held my tongue with her teeth a millisecond longer, and then released. It stung a bit, but it quickly dissipated. She quickly soothed it with her tongue. This unpredictable dance goes on for while. We are both unsure when it will end, but neither wanted to end it. Her initial slowness in momentum would quickly follow with a rapid pace. "Had she done this before?"

Hey! I thought you were no random! She asked, chuckling at the whimsical look that grazed my face.

I know nothing of this girl. She knows nothing of me. I raised my head up to take in some much-needed oxygen from the tarred air.

We should go inside now. They might be looking for us. She said.

Yes, you are right! I am crazy after all, and they would be smart to worry. She chuckled at the phrase.

I led while she followed. We made our way through the jubilant crowd and aimed for the northernmost part, the area where we were last seen. We brushed past a number of joyous revellers too consumed by their emotions. I looked back and she is doing the just fine, following in my wake, paddling like ducks on water.

 Hey dude, where have you been? Totally disappeared! Anton broke from behind the crowd. He hadn't noticed Eloise.

Eloise interjected.

He slightly puzzled. He must have thought.

''Who was she?'' "Where had she come from?" I, on the other hand, knew her well physically but little else, a student from Finland on Pat's program.

 Hi, I am Anton.

Sorry, this is Anton, my buddy from the hostel. We share the same dorm.

 Hey, Anton! Hi, am Eloise.

 Nice to meet you.

Nice to meet you too. I see.

You are Swedish!!!! She chuckled hard.

I could feel a light tap on my left shoulder. Someone was attempted to grab my attention, but doing a poor job of it. In the midst of getting re-acquainted with Anton, I am doing a thrilling job of introducing Eloise with how little I knew.

Yes, she is Finish and yes, she is here to study just like you.

I was reiterating for Anton's sake. He seemed to have been taken by Eloise too.

I felt another attempt, again very lightly, very politely. I turned around to be greeted by Tae-Song and Min-Jae, the two Koreans that had helped me find the G-guest house.

Whoa! You are one popular guy! How long did you say you have been here? Eloise enquired.

Well, less than 13 hours and counting, to be precise! Whoa! How do you know those two? They look like locals. She whispered.

They saw me struggling on my way in from Itaewon and helped me find my hostel.

Oh cool, you must have a friendly face.

Well, people do tend to tell me this.

Just as they were narrow and beauteous on Namdaemun, a pair of perfectly woven paramour, with much accord it would seem, Min-Jae, entrusted the bulk of her welt to Tae-Song and he held on to it strong broadchested.

The pair hardly exchanged a word, just subtle glances. The silence only a smile could carry with much delivery.

I could see many questions marred across their acute faces, but they said little. Even did little else but gestured to Eloise's prying.

My Korean acquaintances disappeared into the midst with as little as a nod goodbye. Anton was gone too. I had thought about making plans for later, but this had been missed. He had allowed himself to be swallowed by the crowd and Eloise held lead us right into it.

Her lower back was moist from the heat, me at her waistline, her slender frame right in proportion to mine. Our heads intimately met gently, my eyes closed, I could sense her innermost thoughts and she could mine, in sync as though we harmonically conversed, rhythmic to the music that filled the room.

These were humid moments, ones we shared out at the smoking area. She pulled at my vest in a bid to lower my head. Successfully, she gained at her quest and I found my lips locked tight with hers. Efficiently, she uses her tongue again to tease, manipulate, and lure. She bit my tongue and held it, this time, a lot longer than she had done outside. I paused for a moment, unable to move, tensed at this very act. I attempted to say something but could barely utter a word as she had my tongue held at ransom. For a moment or two I could hardly decide whether this was fun or foul play.

We broke for a moment, her eyes still locked with mine. I am certain she was just as done with the crowd, her hands firmly placed in grasp as we borrowed through the thick of it. Once outside, still dark, streets filled with revellers bidding an early retreat at the taxi rank. She pulled at me once again, slag at the herms of my vest. Its elasticity quickly dissipated and I could feel the night's breeze working its way more easily through.

We could go back to mine? she said softly, which sent tingles through my lopes equally as she was taking charge. We stopped by a late night Korean ramen kitchen where every seat occupied by a local. We were early enough with a few minutes wait for a table. We surveyed the chalk written menu that hung from a wall above a counter.

We took in the many broth soup options on the menu and settled for one to share between us.
"Haejangguk" "Haejangguk" The waitress behind the counter called out to the chefs in the steamy kitchen.

Ulineun geugeos-eul eod-eossda. Ulineun geugeos-eul eod-eossda"

KAMSAMIDA!!!

They called back to her. Pans and utensils racketed away as they chopped, stirred, and flipped.
The aroma from the kitchen had us both salivating enough to intensify the hunger. Eloise looked doe-faced. I wasn't quite sure if it was her being concupiscent or an alcohol-induced hunger and a rampant need to soak it up.

Within a moment or two, the chef had whipped together a rich broth of meaty Oxtail soup. The waitress leaned over as she placed the big bowl on our table, enough broth to feed two.

Jeulgyeo! Enjoy!

Eloise reached for the wooden spoon and whipped up a spoonful.

It's so rich! She said Try it! I grabbed the other wooden spoon and slowly dipped into the leafy meat filled soup and retrieved its steamy piped liquid and quickly placed into my mouth. The heat numbed my tongue. I could hardly differentiate between its liquid and flavour. I got the kick from the savoury after taste. Then, a massive array of beef herb seasoning rushed to hit my taste buds like a wave to a shore.

Wow That's really hot! I said.

Across the room was a face I recognized but could not quite place. As I slurped, she looked intensely at me. It was familiar. It wasn't Areum or Hye's, nor was it Tae-Song's pale faced girlfriend Min-Jae. It had been a familiar one that I was sure I knew, but couldn't quite place.

We took a corridor that lit up with every step, I paid little attention to the lady that took her terrier out for a walk. it nocturnally sauntered around in a bid to do a bit of foraging in the hedges. With Eloise's chin gently held in my hand, I lifted it to meet contentiously with a kiss. She held my bottom and pulled me into her quickly. She kissed back, equally competitive, and thrusted her waist back and forth. She bit at the tip of my lip and withdrew.

I am engulfed between her legs, unable to move like a python's grip of its host – the eventual squeeze and crush. She swallowed me between her trimmed thighs until I ran out of patience and her persistent urged me to break free.

I pushed aside her legs with one little effort and she succumbed. I reached for her thighs and lifted them high. She is two feet off the carpeted floor. Her red black pattern concealed her behind decently but gave access to my hands.

We motioned ourselves in an awkward symbiotic manner. I fed ravenously on her lips and she hustled comfortably in my arms. A few walk down the hall with my hands well hidden underneath her dress. I felt her soft, smooth skin. She decided to disembark from the comfort I had provided.

For a second or two, she pulled away and leaned against the wall. She stared at me seductively but said nothing, just stared intensely. I decided to play along and leaned against the opposing wall facing opposite of her. She stood a meter or two apart, her index finger in her mouth. She sucked on it and winked at me. She pulled her supposedly moist finger out of her mouth and worked it down her beautiful landscape of contrasted peaks and eventually into her valley where it disappeared within the thin vales of her cottoned fabric. I watched her play and toil away, not knowing what wonders she summoned down below to evoke such unhindered emotion. An expression sat upon her face, so deeply conveyed, very passionately every single unseen stroke.

I had to intervene, not only because someone could walk in on her at a moment notice, but also because I had been ceremoniously jealous. How was she so capable of getting herself pent up to enjoy such pleasures? Quite frankly, I had started to feel a bit left out.

She reached out her hand and pulled me in slowly. She kissed me welcomingly, then thrusted her moist finger deep into my mouth. I thought for a second about where it had been a minute ago. I could taste its salty fluid. She kissed with suction which quickly took away the taste.

That slow paced rhythmic strut got much more audible, and we could tell someone was on their way up. Whoever it was, they got closer with every step. We could do without an interruption — as much as it would be exhilarating to show off. A few more steps up those creaked stairway and we were within grasp of being caught.

Eloise had lost her shoes. She held them, dangling in her right hand, and walked barefoot with her black undergarment in her other. We shut the door to her apartment just before the strut made it to us. With her back against the door, the kissing continued as if our two lips had been long missed and were catching up on old times. We heard the strut walk pass her door and decelerate. Eloise could not contain herself any longer, but chuckled at the absurdity.

The strut quickly paced away and disappeared up a flight of stairs. We pulled at each other, kissed and shoved around her small studio., We knocked over unwashed pots with a large metallic crash. She had left them out on the side. Neither of us stopped to acknowledge the spill over. I imagined it to be an absolute mess.

I found myself with my back to her foam. Its irregular surface, there were other things there. It felt like her clothing was accompanying us. I shoved at them from behind and she joined in.

Sorry! I was not expecting anyone, her first words uttered in minutes.

She reached for the top drawer to her right next to the study.

You should put this on.

Once again, I was acquainted with the humid heat of the subtropical South Korean peninsula.

I sweat and she sweats as we made at it. In a world of our own, she groaned and scratched my back. I, on the other hand, carefully place mine between the arches of her back. I thought of nothing else at this very moment but to be present, consumed by the intense sensation between both our limbs as she jolted intermittently between our rhythmic flow.

Wow I am exhausted! Would you like some water? Oh yes please, sure!

She got up at one point and revealed a full display of her bare perky bottom.

I can't believe I just hit that. I thought to myself. This is one lucky day. All is well with life. I am in an entirely new continent. I have a new life, am a new man, and I am winning even if it's going to be short-lived. It is as it is a life lived.

Eloise returned with two glasses, the water chilled, poured from the tap. She handed one over to me. This human connection I am certain has very little potential to blossom. Yet, it is beautiful as we sit opposed in stark nudity. She will be here for another year or so I will be back home in a weeks.

"If only I could stay."

And so, and so, my mind pattering went on. I almost forget to enjoy the present moment. I am worried sick of losing her, whatever it was we had managed to come upon. I do not know how to build upon it.

"Such chicken shit."

Eloise leaped knees apart on top. Instinctively, I grabbed at her. Her arms prevented her recoil to the ground. She lunged at my neck, kissing and biting. I enjoyed her feast, doing nothing but relishing the weight of her nude body mounted on me.

She opened the windows on her way back and the night's fresh breeze soothed well. Both of us were exhausted. Finally, she made her way to my lips. We interloped, tongues wrestling in a bid to out muscle. We danced and teased with no real motive, but to please. We were soon back at it, humping until the morning dawned on us.

That familiar face, the one from the noodle kitchen? It was Nari's she had recognized me.

Chapter 10

Garosugil:

Sunday 10:13 am Seoul South Korea 2015: The fresh morning dew of the Gingko trees could be felt as we stepped out of apartment 54b. A drop hits my forehead, and then another. At first, I wondered *''had a cloud formed suddenly above us?''* The bright blue skies of the morning could very well be gone, and now dark grey clouds, thick as an otter's fur, were about to break loose with heavy precipitation.

I wiped my forehead with my right palm, felt the cold wet sensation that had suddenly formed. There are no clouds up there, just the bright blue skies, still as clear as we had seen them earlier, looking through the small circular windows, arched at a 45 degrees angle, the most give the glass window gave to opening outwards.

I was enamoured by the bright golden colours, that lined the broad streets, that distinctive acrid smell of butyric acid that lingered long in the air, putting us off, and the slippery pavement of dead leaves on which we gingerly walked. The autumn bloom of the Gingko trees had arrived, the first fall of its foliage.

She grabbed hold of my hand with her fingers fit snuggly between mine, similar to the way the ginkgos were interwoven. Like regular couples taking a leisurely stroll on a crisp Sunday morning, we walked and walked, surveying the cityscape. I realized I had been in Korea for less than 13 hours. My flight landed in the humid afternoon heat the day before, now, here I was, almost settled in. I walked the pavement, adoring the lined golden trees and the city's contemporary ultra-modern architecture, cool trendy cafes, — from book cafes to Iguana cafes, cat cafes to owl cafes. It seemed an idea with a pint of cute had to be made into a café.

In the midst of a populated street, it's steep, quite easily inclined at a 39-degree angle and laden with graffiti art. Most of the Korean BBQ restaurants located on this particular street were closed. Sure, it's way too early to have any either way. The closed signs were positioned evidently on the front doors, centred in the middle and in black ink, "CLOSED!"

What would you fancy, a coffee, something to eat? The night before had been long and attenuated. Crave gratifying. Sex several times over and over. I got the impression she had few sexual partners before then.

I can do with a coffee right about now Yes, me too. She said. We should look for one, that's really weird. It's South Korea after all. She said. I think we will find one quite easily here. too right! I replied. Hey, what about that one? She asked.

We walked towards the wood-panelled shop. Its oak wood finish stood out from the neighbouring shops. Again the same sort; mum and pop's, medium-sized convenience.

A growing queue had formed outside its entrance, mainly locals. A small group of Japanese tourist conversed in Japanese. A quick glance at the menu on display outside the café displayed the regular caffeinated offerings, a breakfast menu, and pastries and ice creams. Only this time, you got to enjoy it with a pet raccoon.

Wow, a raccoon café! Now that's interesting. We ought to check this out, even if it is for one drink.

Eloise grabbed hold of my left hand the way that she did the night before, reassuringly refreshed. I looked back to catch her gaze, she was just as doe-eyed as they were several hours before, tired and sparkled.

The waitress approached us with a broad smile, twinkle in her eye, and an expectant sense of excitement.

Hello, Hello, The waitress greeted.

Annyeonghaseyo! She added.

 Annyeonghaseyo! We repeated back to her as we stepped into the tavern.

Smartly dressed, she asked us.

Where would you like to sit, sir?

We were both still very much taken in by the place, an old Hanok house converted right in the middle of the city. It's a heavy oak wood build, with white walls and transparent sliding doors, that lead to different compartments.

You can sit over here, or anywhere you like. She suggested.

Are you okay with this one? The waitress asked.

Eloise was more taken with the presence of a raccoon that pottered about the café.

So, have you been here before? The waitress inquired.

Okay, I will give you some background on our café. As you know, we run a raccoon café here. They are usually in the pen, but sometimes you can see them roaming around. Yes, like that one over there Luigi!

So cute! Eloise interjected.

They do not bite, so you will be safe! They do not spread rabies either. Both have had injections. She stated.

Oh, that's good to know. I don't want to have to get rabies. Eloise muttered under her breath.

The café had its own secret garden, with a well-manicured lawn, pebbled and stone slab trail, trimmed junipers, a small pond, and a patio styled wooden deck — a sort of miniaturized hidden oasis engulfed in the middle of the Hanok. It was a grand eastern courtyard, if you like.

It once belonged to an 18th-century Korean socialite, an aristocrat. The waitress went on She acquired it as a gift from her lover and spent most of her last years living here.

We sat at the table set for two, close to the wall, opposite the garden. A smile so well practiced perhaps, well over a thousand times into a mirror. It's just too coherent. perfectly formed an oval display of her perfectly set teeth.

''*That million dollar smile.*'' The thought quickly crossed my mind. I have seen this same smile before.'' Yes that's it Melanie's', that excellent smile, infectious, seductively alluring. It douses you with a pretence of innocence.

"*Fools are those that believe smiles are a sign of happiness.*"

Paula Acedo- (Goodreads)

So, I literally know nothing about you. She said.

Well, I wouldn't say that. You do know a thing or two, and I could say the same for you too, I know nothing! I said.

That's not such a bad thing. She said.

Oh! Wow

Just saying, the less you know, the better for you. She said.

Oh okay, what do you mean by that then? I asked.

So, how long did you say you're staying in Seoul for? She asked.

Well, I have got four nights in this city, then I'll decide what to do next. I've only been here less than a day.

A few hours? She enquired.

Yea, that will be less than 16 hours I still haven't had a full day here yet. I responded.

Wow! You're doing very well! She said.

And what do you mean by that? I asked.

I mean you're clearly a lucky guy. She added

Not sure what you mean?" I added.

Just saying... hmmm! she added.

So, how do you know Patrick? She asked.

Patrick! Oh, we were on the same flight in from Beijing. Interesting guy! I said.

Wow, you're just a walking poster boy for randomness Ah! So, how often do you travel on your own? She asked.

At this point, I am contemplating her train of thought. Suddenly she had become acutely interested. We had spent a good amount of time outside in the smoking area talking of pretty much everything, from the insightful to the humane. An ample amount of body chemistry and an insouciant attitude had led to the most intimate of moments. Only now does it occur to her, we barely knew each other. Her reasoning seemed an inverse to the norm. She is still here and I am too.

Well! I am doing this particular trip on my own. At times I do travel with friends, typically around Europe.

Oh Okay! She uttered.

How about you? I asked.

Well, I did, a lot around South East Asia, a few years ago. That trip, I was on my own. I went to Cambodia, Philippines, Laos, and Thailand. Backpacked mostly, spent some time working with charities in Cambodia,

Oh brilliant. I stated.

Yes, it was, very rewarding, hard work, through. She added.

I bet. I uttered.

To be frank, it is nothing new.

"Aha!"

To think of it. I am actually on my own here too, but it's to study."

So how did you meet Patrick then? I asked.

International relations! We're in the same course, remember? she said.

Yea! That's it.

We met at the new students meeting. He really stood out in a Finnish sort of way, although I know he is German. What do you mean Finnish sort of way? I can't quite explain it, but I do know what I mean. We just clicked. It might just be a Nordic thing. She said.

I mean, I do speak a bit of German too. I am half Finnish, half German. Did I tell you this? She asked.

She pulled away at her blonde locks, partially covering her face.

No, you didn't. Come to think of it, you didn't say much either.

Well, what the fuck did we talk about then? She asked.

Lots of body language?

I guess. She said.

And Soju!

Yes, Soju! she said with a hint of laughter.

Who was that old man at the clubhouse? I asked.

Which old man?

Well, the one with the slender Korean lady?

Oh him. She said. Well, he is one of the lecturers and that slender lady would be his wife. She added.

I thought I recognized him from the Airport. I mentioned.

Yes, that would be accurate too. He also arrived just in time for the start of the semester, Prof Duszynski, Head of International Business Studies at the Gyeongsang National University. He is Polish-American. She said.

Underneath the table was one of the raccoons. It's bushy greyish black tail drifting about, bit by bit, in and around the legs of the table. It had been attempting to sniff out whatever food we had on our plates. It pottered around and lifted its nose every few minutes at it drew closer. It positioned itself behind Eloise, who was totally oblivious to the little Procyon's movement. Suddenly, it climbed the water pole, mounted the wall in haste, and jumped right on Eloise's head in absolute pandemonium.

"Get it off me!" "Get it off me!" She cried out in a shock.

It's okay! It's okay! Harmless, Harmless. The waitress urged.

The raccoon quickly jumped into her arms for nuts the waitress presented to it.

My goodness, it had me there. She said.

Are you okay?

Yea! I think we should go somewhere else. She suggested.

Sure, if it makes you feel safer.

Yea! She added.

We walked out with the two waitresses apologizing efficaciously for the mishap.

"It never happened before", "So sorry!", "So sorry." She uttered. You could tell they were really concerned,

I think it really liked you there. I added.

You think so? She asked.

Yea, it came over to say hello. Teasing her.

So it jumped on my head? She stated.

I think that's how they play.

You don't know anything about raccoons. She added.

No I don't, but they seem like very friendly little things.

Well, I don't think it was being friendly at all. It wanted my bingsu. She stated.

We walked out and continued down Yongsan-gu, walking the many narrow paths. Lots of neon Korean Calligraphy adjoined to sides of buildings. At 11:25am in the morning, all of the choreograph lights were out, they were simply plaques with names of numerous businesses lined on the steep lane. We walked passed a nail shop and Eloise ventured in.

Standing in wait, I am suddenly far away, deep in thought as deserted as an Arabian desert. I am lost in a cluster that fogs my mind. I just about made out my own reasoning.

Aniko's text had arrived late last night, round about the time we made for Eloise's studio.

"Hey Ray, How are you doing?
It's lovely here in Busan. Arrived a few hours ago.
Hope all is going well in Seoul?
* X"*

Sounds like she is doing just fine, I thought through the breezy feel of her message.

"Hey, Aniko all is well ☺ Send.
* It has been non-stop fun in here. Send*
Hope your adventure is going well?
Chat soon Ray x." Send.

Eloise emerged from the shop and I am delighted. I hadn't encouraged her and she had picked up the hint. I had no real interest in hanging around.

Did you find anything you liked? Not really, I might come back, there are a few things I would like to try. She said.

Those whinny lanes with a legion of contemporary shop stores. They all seemed to go in different directions. The path was flat and plain until we hit a steep hill and discovered some more of the same, these meaningless wonder round strange lands with my new acquaintance.

I pulled out my phone to take a picture of an interesting looking Buddha, perfectly at peace in face, neither frowning nor smiling. An expression of absolute contentment welcomed passerby to its secluded building behind. We figured it a monastery, one for the monks.

This cloister was positioned on top of the hill oversee the city at such a spot that you could gaze long over the breath-taking view below it. "It truly is a beauty!"

In complete silence, we stand and we look outward onto the many enclaves of the city. Those twinkling from headlights in the traffic below, even in broad daylight. The reticent monastery was behind us and the bustling city ahead. The two very contrasted energies were so different, it left me feeling connected and appeased in the moment.

 Does any of this have any meaning, *"any relevance, "* *"or just another subconscious mind map to construct meaningful outpost of a simple casual existence?"*

Everyone down there is on a mission to somewhere, to something: maybe a trip to work, a visit to see a family member, pregnant women on her way to delivery, a couple's weekend break away. There just so much happening down there and all at the same time.

Eloise stood back up and took a picture of the landscape. She got me with my back facing outwards.

Oh, that's quite a shot! She muttered, and I only noticed she had taken it when her shutter went off again.

It's a good shot, one for your profile. She added.

Let me see that please?

Sure! You know people from Finland are quite shy?

We tend to avoid eye contact, not because we are being rude. It's just how we are. She added.

Yea, I kind of noticed that earlier. Can I tell you something? She asked.

Yea, sure!

I mean you're not going to judge me by it? She asked.

Yea, sure. I am not going to judge you. Now what is it?

I kind have not been with a black guy before. She muttered.

Okay! Have you been with anyone before? I asked.

Silly! That's for me to know.

Well, you volunteered the info, and I kind of guessed too.

Guessed what? She asked.

Well, the black guy thing.

Ohh!

Your skin is soo smooth I like it. she muttered.

Chapter 11

Unicorn:

The heartbreak came heavy like a trump from a jazz piece. First, the subtle melodies of the cello, then, the fiddly keys of the piano carefully lead on. Note by note, you take it in.

The careful drum-like percussion of the double bass to which you found comfort, you bumble along to its deep and short minor tone. Reassuringly disguising it's very pain within.

Her symphony of grand adversity, you are enticed by its surface, the smooth shiny keys of the Piano as smooth as skin she liked. It played in suspended fourth, its perfect! You fall, omitted like the major third, you ignore your own very instincts *"GET THE FUCK OUT!"*

They had served you well this whole time, but for some reason, it seem to come against the one very thing you want the most: *"The Lust"*, *"Her Companionship" and "The Association."*

She knew this is why you stuck around, playing her keys like the mid-tempo, her low tempo dazzling you along, pulling not just your energy, but others, just as hopelessly enamoured as you. Cleverly, she masks her chaotic flaw like a diminishing arpeggio. She is broken yet beautiful.

A hot mess in every sense of the word, yet childishly disregarded, you horned onto her sweet tones. The major, the minor, the augmented, all seem to be well so orchestrated. You bask in the glory of winning her trophy.

A broken one at that, although little known to you, played like the suspended fourth. You omitted and replaced versions of events with much more self-serving ones. Then comes the trumpet, spawned at full throttle, speaking its truth over the melodies you have gotten so well accustomed too. You are threatened as it's a new sound, louder and realistic. It doesn't fit well with the carefully constructed fib you both created, more so, the one you told yourself.

Now that she broke out, and did so in not so much of an argumentative manner but as a matter of fact. "This is who I am!" or "What I am!" take it or leave it. "So sorry I was misleading, I was just as equally bemused by it all, unsure of what I really wanted." The long and short of it, "It's not working out." You have to go or better yet "We can't see each other anymore."

You took it, as it was, not fully sure what it is you have just heard, not fully sure what it is you did taken on, you just do. The shock of it all, the quick realization what it might mean, the not being affected by it in the moment, and then like the pitch of a flute piped, it hits and suddenly dawns on you. You're in shock.

In your head, you heard it over and over again, the same tune but at a much different octave. It is much more poignant the more you play it back, especially as she isn't here to deliver it in person.

There is no hope to convince her that she made a catastrophic mistake. Only she really isn't, it is you and has been you all along, tortured poor soul, refused to give it up. Blew up every single sentence every word like a Bernoulli at high flute pitch.

We can't be together any more! She said.

Each one had hit hard, a millisecond apart for good measure. Your mind is your friend and yet your worst enemy in a good sequence. You knew exactly how to exert the pain, torture at ease, and pleasure worse than the orchestrator. You burn, you live with the pain, mad, not at your mind but at the orchestrator. "*You did this to me!*" Not knowing the classics, it never gets old.

"I am just so hungry!" She returned to tapping away on her smartphone, thoroughly consumed by whatever it was that was that captivated her from the other side of the line. We had taken the night flight out. It's Paris cold and wet, the North Western wind reassuringly chilly. I can just about see the Louvre to the left of her shoulder, protected by nothing but a dark cropped biker jacket which she wore snuggly. A silk shirt hugged her loosely, displaying her asserts well as she reclined deeply into a wooden bistro chair.

We can go somewhere else if you don't like it here? She looked up, both eyebrows arched at an instant. "Oh, nice!" She responded with her trademark remark of disinterest.

The waiter came over with a silver tray well anchored above his left shoulder. A lonely porcelain plate sits in the middle and he is accompanied with a look of bewilderment. This grazed his face, as if to say; *"You are dining alone, yet you're out with her?"*

He gave his last and final attempt to win her over Madam mademoiselle, Is there anything I can get you? He asked and it is in vain. He sunk his head a few inches lower into his gaunt shoulders, a gesture of bemusement again *"Whatever is wrong with her?"*

We had been down this road earlier at the hotel lobby, a few hours after a gloomy elevator ride down, and at the coffee shop on Rue de Babylone- no joy there. At bakery shop on St Germain des Pres- hopeless! Another attempt, on Rue Monge- was a shamble. I cajoled with no hint of a win in sight. I am hungry, very hungry, yet too proud to share this with her. We had been on the same flight in, a total 214 miles from London. In the midst of the rush, we had skipped dinner and hopped right onto the plane. The taxi ride had been more miserable than a baboon's backside. The frost of the cold mirrored her temperament precisely, like twins with telepathic tendencies. "What is the point of it all?"

The endless bickering, back and forth *"I really don't want to go."* I feel I pressed her to. *"I am so sorry!"* I pressed her to come along.

"I pressed you to come along."

I suppose I desired every mug she threw at me. She didn't want to be here in beautiful, romantic Paris, She didn't want to be here, at least not with me, yet here we were. We sat opposite one another with no single word to utter in an ersatz solace.

The tapping returned, only this time more frivolously. I crackled through dinner, she battled with the screen. She pressed every button as fast as she could. She couldn't wait to get her message across. Whoever it was on the other side was just as frivolous. Messages were streaming in thick and fast. I gathered this was the case by the pace at which her smartphone repeatedly emitted its tinkle—every new message accompanied by a prompt tinkle.

I couldn't wait to be done with dinner. I stuffed the creamy based risotto down my gob as quick as I could, an Italian classic in a very French bistro—what a mix match!

That's What Happens: "Clever you, Sadistic me. You think you've won, But you don't see, The sinister plot I've laid for thee. Clever you, Sadistic me."

Poet Author: Kissy Marie 2014
https://hellopoetry.com/Kissy-Marie/

"Are you okay?" Her sudden concern took me by surprise. *What does she care?* If she gave a damn ,she would at least show some courtesy at dinner. Better yet, do away with the bloody phone and engage with me. Perhaps we should take a walk around town after dinner? I suggested. I figured this would be a great chance to get some air and re-equilibrate—a chance to think things over. Maybe the sceneries of beautiful Paris would win her over. She could finally get over her misery and enjoy the trip.

Dark as it was, the streets were well lit. I felt we might have been transported back to the medieval. We walked through the cobbled streets, past the Notre Dame. She is still saying very little : an occasional "*Yes that will be fine,*" an "*Oh nice!*" now and again, which I have known too well to indicate disinterest. She is paying very little attention in regards to my suggestions, as I cautiously hint as to whether a certain tourist hotspot would be worth visiting.

At this point, I notice how weak in character I had become. It left me utterly vulnerable and open to her tinkering. "*I am not taking full charge of this.*" I would say to myself, over and over, as we walked the dark streets. "*This isn't going to end well,*" I would tell myself in an almost self-prophetic mantra.

I am full of fear, not wanting to admit my severe desire for attachment. She is unengaged, indifferent, and constantly avoiding any slight chance of intimacy.

A jazz piece comes to mind: Miles Davis's "*Feio,*" that airy unsettling of the trumpets, the rattling drums interceding between keys of an electric piano and a guitar. The distant dog barking leaves you with a chill, a rumble in my belly, as if the music was being composed and played right at the bottom of my gut. "*The diary of a weak man's game!*" with just one thought, one thought only that lingered at the back of my mind. "*How can I turn this around?*" I managed to accomplish such a task in the past winning her over, again and again, only this time I am certain it is final. I am equally frustrated and fee up with her farce.

We walked the Pont des Art with previous intentions of a lovelock tie, throwing the small keys into the slow running river Seine. While kissing passionately, I would have her with her back to the Institute de France. Any slight temptations about opening her eyes as we kissed will be met with the sight of an enchanting large glass pyramid to heighten the romance. I had thought about this as we sat at the café on St-Germain-des-Pres overlooking the Palace, but "Il n'y a pas d'amour ici," just the chilling wind of the north-western hemisphere. We stroll with just the comfort of my dark humour to console me. "*Elle va être seule. Seule pour longtemps.*" I would say to myself smugly as she walked the cobbled road leading towards the Saint Germain Des Pres Quarter.

I would ponder over a parallel universe when she was truly mine again, and me hers. Longing that if things had been great between us she did be reaching to grab hold of my hand as we walked the dimly lit streets. So was my thinking and looking back now, I had gotten it totally wrong. No one belongs to anyone. The concept itself is flawed. That same reasoning was the bane of my anxiety. But, it took for me to lose her, and go through the pain, before self-actualizing.

Chapter 12

Delayed:

Saturday 08: 12 am Beijing PEK Airport 2015:
Running as fast as my legs would carry me. Lifted,
pounced as lightly as possible, My foot hits the
ground and sprung almost immediately, getting as
much lift from every stride.

I dragged on the TULLY and it behaved well,
smoothly in fact, as it rolled and twisted in every
direction. My hands instinctively waved it. KEG the
backpack jittered along, strapped to my back. This
time, I added extra tightening to its straps to keep it
from making a racket whilst strapped. It weighed
even heavier than usual now. Purchased goods from
the oriental store had added a few more pound.
Although I am certain it would still pass the 7kg
carry on baggage limit imposed by the airline.

The check-in area was packed, a massive queue
ahead as I ran towards it in-between the many
bystanders, The crowd began to thicken. I broke
through as inconvincible a gap as the crowd
presented.

 Cuse me! Cuse me! here and there Cuse me ! I
bumped into the crowd, made sure the TULLY,
wasn't doing as much havoc as I was.

I narrowly avoided an elderly couple. A brief sigh to my relieve, my trajectory pushed me into the path of a group, of slow-moving travellers that walked the Airport's foyer. The PEK had a relatively vast foyer size. The mile-long run in, from the taxi rank, took me a total 25 minutes, to reach the Cathy Pacific's Airlines check-in desk.

Large information monitors beamed with little fonts, displaying numerous minute data on scheduled flights In and out of the PEK that morning. Neatly listed accordingly, inbound flights on the right, outbound on the left. A quick stop at one of this monitor revealed my flight to Seoul was still on time, this gave another sigh of relieve. At first, it wasn't up there as I scanned rapidly, twice and then a third time over, to make sure nothing had been missed. The moving tab kept rolling, changing from destination to destination with no listing for Seoul. Eventually, it got displayed in bright yellow-mustard colours.

Time: 08: 12 am Flight No: CA972 Cathy Airlines To: Seoul S. Korea Gate No: Wait in lounge.

Eventually, I got my turn at the check-in desk, slightly out of it, but with great anticipation to the Odyssey ahead. Gradually, I regained consciousness, my breathing returned back to its normal respiratory rate.

Hi there!

She spoke in a very soft, professional and poised manner.

Hello I responded.

Can I have your passport and booking details please? She requested.

Sure!

I put forward the folded paper, printed from the log's front desk. The ink strayed down the side of the paper and this, I found all of a sudden to be very embarrassing. Either its cartridge had been faulty or it was low on the pigmented substrate. The text was very faint and difficult to comprehend.

I can just about see it. It's not a very good print. She flicked at the paper, almost sending flying across her counter.

I know, I had one done in a haste. I guess the printer must have been low on ink. At the log I mean. I remarked.

It's okay. I can make it out. She said.

Her fingers dashed across the keyboard below the counter. Her eyes firmly glued to the screen, arched to the side of her. She looked and strained her eyes at the paper, flicking it hard as if the print would sudden appear bolder as she handled it.

Seoul!

She said and I responded, almost immediately.

Yes!

She strained again at the paper, very quickly this time, and returned to some more typing.

08: 12 am flight time! Okay, let me have your passport, please? She requested.

My passport slid insistently across the attendant's raised counter. She picked it up and immediately flipped to its back pages. She slid its radio-chipped page onto the side of her monitor, after which she returned to some more typing, striking at her keyboard as promptly as humanly possible. All along her, eyes were glued onto radiating screen, tonnes of light photons smashed right to the back of her iris. Her reading glasses might have taken some of the edges off. She sat up close to the screen.

How many bags are you checking in? She asked. ''Just the one !''

I motioned TULLY onto the hard rubber surface and immediately, she slapped on an adhesive tag with a serial code 7670002325CA, my flight number: CA972, last name ''Decosta'' destination ''SEL''. I watched as TULLY swiftly disappeared, riding the conveyer belt into the abyss, a dark hole. One thought stayed with me : the hope to reunite again with the black box-shaped traveller case.

The KEG was still very much strapped to my back and reassuringly so. It was loaded with spares, the sort of things to keep occupied and a number of toiletries to keep from being refreshed. Essentials for long hauls and worst case scenario, a survival pack.

She printed out rectangular tickets from a machine below and tucked it in between the pages of my passport Seat K20, was visible as she stretched out her arm to hand it back to me.

Enjoy your flight to Seoul. She said with a customary smile.

I motioned myself through the air-conditioned foyer. The crowd had grown and was growing even bigger at a faster pace with every passing minute. The daunting feeling of being in a large public space stream with thousands of people, going somewhere, coming from someplace or simply saying their goodbyes. Oh, the magic of travel. I am embedded deep in the midst of my wanderlust.
I can't quite wait to leave this space of enormous commuter energy, can't quite wait to embark on another thrilling adventure to the one I had just completed. The trails up the Great Wall, taking in the magnificent views of the steep forested mountains. My mind wandered just as well and I let it, with this much time to kill, I can indulge in a bit of wanderlust.

The PEK is a very large airport, sat in the departure lounge. The big airplanes line its aprons, ready for the next flight out. You could just about see the staff scuffled with the cargos as they unloaded one plane. Mechanics in beach blue overall walked around inspecting its engines and body. Flashlights protruded through its dark greasy jets.

Suddenly it hits me, I looked around and saw hoards of mid-twenty something Chinese, Africans and western travellers in queues. ''There is a huge influx of tourists here.'' It's September the 5th. Two weeks exploring the rural Chinese villages of Jiuzhaigou and Yunnan. Both south-western Sichuan province of China. Yunnan's beautifully caved out rice paddy on mountainsides, filled with water, reflecting skies and clouds in colourful hues of blue and turquoise. The waterfalls of Jiuzhaigou valley drumming down tonnes into its crystal clear glacial lake that laid stoic a few miles down its trail.

 The villages had gotten me accustomed to seeing quite a monolith indigenous demographic. The PEK was a far contrast from that, a sort of show reel depiction of the globalization and tourism interest in China.

I thought of a way to kill time, still with no gate number to Cathy Pacific's flight CA972. The yellow mustard fonts still read "Wait in lounge." As a default I resorted to scrolling on the Old Oliver. Something transient would do just fine for the moment. "Marian- Only our hearts to lose" track listing "Passengers" The deep haunting humming sounds of the vocal, interestingly calm, streamed in. Every line to the lyric tentatively resonant as I sat there and listened.

"Nobody knows where it goes." He sings in his husky voice.

"We are passengers to nowhere."

The intermittent sharp high-pitched harmony intercepted ever so often, it re-enforced the song's haunting ambiance. I sat and soaked it up, seemingly reflecting on what the point was of embarking on such an unconventional journey. 15 minutes went by pretty quickly as I sat there on the lightly padded metal bench.

At 7:55 am the flight's gate number should be up there, I thought to myself. The KEG backpack served well as footrest. I grabbed it from the floor and mounted to my back, walking the short radius of the information board with the yellow-mustard fonts displayed:

Flight No: CA972 Airline: Cathy Pacific Destination: Seoul S Korea Gate No: Delayed.

Oh Bagger !!!

———

That euphoric feeling, a synonym for travel, was suddenly gone. The rush for the Odyssey had been all in vain. Running through the crowded foyer, whizzing in-between clusters, contending with slow-moving travellers and their large travel cases. When I almost knocked over an elderly gentleman holding his white Pekingese as he bids his wife farewell, all had been in vain. "Oh bagger !"

KEG was now off my back, one hand held its top loop as it slouched to the ground. I pondered on what possible cause for the delay.

"It could be only for few minutes or maybe a couple hours ?" "I can't be certain." A number of other travellers started to congregate below the information board. The same sort of bewilderment that grazed my face earlier could be seen on theirs.
Some chatted in Chinese. I couldn't be sure what was said but it sure was of disappointment.

With no gate number to go to, the next possible option would be to return to the Cathy Pacific's information desk, but that was going to be an impossible task due to the airport's stringently observed security checks. I thought of the TULLY and whether or not it had been properly loaded on.

The lightly padded bench was once again my place of refuge. I attempted to get as comfortable as possible. With no explainable reasons being offered for the delay, we were lagged a good 45 minutes behind scheduled flight for Seoul.

The Old Oliver was, sure enough a good companion at times of distress, I strolled once again through its glassy interface. I want something uplifting this time, only nothing quite cuts it. Most songs seemed to revel in heartbreak, a good proportion, on some sort liberation and then there was Michael Buble's Christmas selection "Santa Claus is coming to town." A single downloaded as a result of Melanie's insistent request. A drive playlist we put in the rotation as we made the hour-long drive to her folks for Christmas 05.

None of the old anamnesis of that year's festivity came back : just the thought of that long sit by the fireplace, fast asleep with Buble's voice in the foreground.

Two hours in and we are still delayed. I am as frustrated as a Cymric house cat. Slouched deep within the seat of a light padded bench situated in the large foyer area the airport offered. It can't be good for the back, but am running out of options. The KEG had served as both pillow and back-rest and, at one point, a foot-rest. Its clunkiness was worse on the back, especially as it had oriental woodwork buried within. The Old Oliver was running low on battery now and at some point, it will need replenishing. It's cord was tucked away deep in the TULLY, rammed beneath tons of other luggage as I suspected. "Oh, the poor Tully! Delusional in thought.

The pressure would be mounted with every baggage deposited crushing it's lined interiors. It's content would be compressed. ''Funny thought'' the same old goods would be manufactured in their millions, each with its own unique serial numbers and perhaps a batch number too. ''Silly me.'', oblivious, christening, each with a name.

So here; TULLY the backpack 26,320 hours that's a total 1day and 18 hours and 3 minutes from tearing its plastic wrapper precisely ! 14 flights, 8 journeys, 6 cities, 3 layovers and 1 delayed flight. No particular reason to it's name it just stuck *TULLY*.

The Old Oliver flickered. Its battery is low and in the red. It still managed to stream out the music and does so with good timbre, to my delight. There is a crowd once again at the information board. It's the bad weather causing the holdup. Torrential gale, the sub-arctic climate, evidently poured down a storm as we sat and watched from the security of large paned, glass windows.

Eventually, the Old Oliver gave up, the ghost and the music quieten. The chatter in Chinese could be heard once again, even louder than before. The frustration could be felt in the air, and reasonably so. That generic chime rang from the public announcement system cutting through the buzz of the crowd so all could hear.

''Cathy Pacific's flight: CA972 Delayed: Due to bad weather.''

We had waited 45 minutes before any information would be given and another hour and a half, waiting for the weather to clear.

I managed through content to which KEG held and felt the presence of a paper, loads of it, stacked in layers, it could only have been from a book, as it is well aligned, thick and layered, papers from the pages of a book. I pulled it out and it was one of the Hemingway's.

"Men Without Women"

 A series of stories on hard men's pageant, unwavering masculinity. It's opening story was themed in central Madrid, Spain. It starts with a bullfighter recovering from an injury, only to yearn for one more blood-thirsty fight with a bull. He is aged, haggard, and out of it, yet he still commands a talent for a dance with his muscular opponent, a beast. He gets his lucky break and fights again, one more fight, one with claws gripping close to fatality. One of the favourites suffered a similar fate (Chaves) and got cogida. At the end, he wins the palaverous fight. Joyously escaping, only just with his life. He is injured badly and once again returned back to the familiar scenes of a hospital bed from which he recovered months before.

"It might just be one of a death delayed, too." I thought to myself.

Speed Date No 3.

So have you done this before? She asked.

She sat there and stared intensely. She doesn't trust me for some reason or another, she just doesn't. Instinctively, some things just don't click and you just know. "It's not going well." Not that it's anyone's fault, it's just compatibility. Four minutes was up and it felt like hours, our tooth pulling conversation came to a blunt end. We endured, more so for the other person's sake, out of courtesy.

So tell me about yourself She added. *"Boring!"* I thought.

The bell goes off and we are both relieved, All the best with your journey. She said. All the best with yours too. I added. An exchange, again, out of courtesy.

I approached table No: 7 and her welcome with a bright dashing smile. I only imagined the last guy had bored her to death, and she was glad to get rid of. Off the beat, she was engaging.

'Nice shoes! She said.

She scribbled down. Oh am just making a note of your number and name. You don't mind, do you? She asked.

Oh no, sure go ahead. I suggested.

Her eyes, inviting, battered her lashes as rapidly as a firecracker's lift off. She stared just as intensely as the girl earlier, as if evaluating.

Is this a prize to be had or forfeit. You did better tell me something interesting.

I imagined this going through her head as she sat, head centred on her mark, which was me.

"And please don't be dull like the last one."

She spoke volumes without uttering a single word. The fabric of her flower-patterned dress barred no grudge with her physique. You could see just how naturally endowed she was in it. Scents of cherries blossomed from a summer morning's harvest, sweet and citrusy. Immediately, I am drawn to my drink on the side. It's a cold. It's a beer, but it will do.

Where were your last travels? She asked.

Budapest! Well, actually Budapest and Transylvania.

Wow, that must have been exciting. How was Transylvania ? It must have been a culture shock! She remarked.

Well a bit. I met some really interesting people there. I added.

I recounted tales of slow, horse-driven carriages as they made their way through the centre of Calea Dorobantilor. The wipe-stroke that contrived the horse to run faster and pulled along its sack cargo, presumably from a local farm. I tell her tales of the smell of cow dung lingering so long in the air that it could be picked up minutes before their arrival and long after they had ridden past.

She wanted to know more about the people I met. ''Why I travelled?'' ''With whom I travelled with mostly?'' ''What sort of places I visited?'' ''Why I choose those places and why not the more obvious one?'' Most curiously, she wanted to know more about the people I had met. Had I formed a uniquely gratifying bond? Would I ever see them again?

And then she got more personal; ''What I did for work?'' ''Where I hanged out?'' When I answered No, she wanted to know ''Why not?''

The bell chimed, 4 minutes was up. The release! I was a caged cat, exasperated. I pounced out of the seat facing No 7 and was more glad to be out of it than I was sitting at table No 6. ''This is exhausting !!!!!''

Chapter 13

Angelic:

18:14 pm Sunday South Korea 2015: That Arabian desert feeling returned. She is very much present, but I am once again lost deep in thought, deep in the fog. I would think in French only to attempt to speak in English, and this became too confusing.

We walked the Garosugil hills back down the city. All the while, Eloise held my hand. It had been an epic view up there as we took in the cityscape, the buildings and slopes of Seoul at night.
Twinkling, from billions of halogen dotted across the cityscape, each from every corner, as far a panoramic a view, our eyes captured. Different hues twinkled at different heights, Perfect strangers moments before, such a sight impacted an emotion on the soul.

She held my hand, but yet, I rattled through the bane of my single-doom, was it due to the fact I hadn't chosen? Or, was I simply imagining my limitations? I pondered as I walked, Eloise right there by my side. She is neither my partner nor friend. I imagined Pat there as he took lots of Polaroids, being over the moon with them. I captured the moment on the black and white film. All 99(W) x 62(H) mm of it, perfectly mirrored on a monochrome frame.

Again I am off beat with the rhythm, lost deep in thoughts. I ought to just enjoy the moment, but for some reason I can't seem to settle. My heart races at a hare's pace.

It was 18:14 pm in the evening, finally a complete full day in Seoul. I am exhausted. It's getting darker and the long walk had taken its toll on both of us.
She spoke very subtly now, maybe because she is equally exhausted. Those uphill battles, literally that's what they were to us. We bonded in the pain. We bonded in the joy of the experience.

Do you reckon you will pay Seoul another visit? She asked.

I don't see why not. It's a heavily cultural place mixing both the new with the old, and it does so seamlessly. I said.

You get to enjoy this for much longer. Yes, of course. I have a year-long study program here.

I plan to see lots of South Korean Daegu, Ulsan close to the south-western coast, Busan and maybe Jeju Island. She added.

You said you were only staying here for 4 days, right? She asked. What else do you plan to see in Korea? She asked.

''*Yes, sure !*'' I thought. I might also do the south-western coast too. I have a friend who is currently starting out by exploring Busan. Well, she is more of an acquaintance really. I stated ''You met on the plane in?'' She asked.

Oh, just like Pat? She asked.

 Yes, well, just like Pat.

Do you meet everyone on the plane these days ? She asked.

Well no, funny of you to mention that, but this will be my first ever experience ever properly connecting to someone on board a plane not to talk of progressive intend on carrying on with it. I stated.

Sure! I met someone once on a plane. She uttered.

Yea?

It was a long time ago. I ended up being a relationship with this person and it lasted quite a long time too. So, maybe this person might be someone special for you. You never know. She added.

Oh, and how about you ? Do you not consider yourself a special person for me ? I asked.

Well… What can I say, we had a good time Ray, and this has been fun, but I don't think I am looking for anything special at the moment. Besides, we will be on opposite sides of the world. I am here for a whole full year. I am not sure I am going to be living in Europe either. She said.

Sure ! This was fun. This is fun ! I added.

The hot pot bubbled away as the heat from the burner went at it. 8 ounces of assorted mushrooms shiitake, crimini, and enoki, bubbled away with the tofu, radish, and napa carrot added earlier to the vegetable broth. We sat and stirred at the stew, oozed its freshly seasoned aroma up our nostrils. We were hungry and I could tell Eloise couldn't wait to get some of the seasoned broth down her.

So what do you think of Pat Polaroids? She enquired.

Oh, those Polaroids? Well, he has a habit of taking a snap of everything. I mean, he ought to be a paparazzi, not an international Business relations person. She stated.

Well to be fair to him, he does have a knack for it. I added.

Twenty minutes of meeting the guy and he was taking a picture of me. Now that's funny weird. She added.

Yeah! Just a bit.

And the old guy with a hot Korean chick? I asked.
Oh you're referring to Prof. Duszynski. She checked
to make sure I was referring to the same man at the
party. Yea, that's him. He was a bit off on the plane. I
added.

Off? She enquired.

Yea, off, but I had to admit I was totally jealous when
I saw him meet up with his younger wife. I added.

No need to be jealous, you too can get an equally
attractive lady too. She stated.

Well, I got you. I mentioned.

Hmmm! Her silence voice quietened at a haste.

The soft tenderness ensured the meat just melted as it
touched my tongue, it was rich in herbs, savoury in
seasoning. The long wait had been worth it. We
stood in line for a table, a slow-moving queue
seemingly, to a well-known hot pot restaurant.
This time around, the feeling was different with us.
When you spend the most part of a day with
someone, it certainly gets you to know them well. It
still remained cordial. We sat, eating and dining, but
there was a certain spirit missing.

" Ah! The spontaneity of it all." That element of surprise, not knowing what's just around the corner. *"That curiosity !"* It's been beaten, a little too hard. *"She literally knows too much."* My guard had been let down, she looked very squarely at me as if she knew something was off. She can't quite put her finger on it.

"It's the spontaneity!" Sure, we were both out of it, more exhausted than a donkey's hind, hungry as we devoured the vegetable-based broth.

"So how long have you been single?" She asked. " Precisely! You mean precisely?" " Well, yeah!" "Like forever!" I said.

"Really?!!" " Well, not really." " Counting my very last which lasted a good six months." "What happened there?" She asked. "Best to leave the past in the past. Besides, it's not good form to talk about one's Ex." " True! True! " She agreed.

" I take it you have been single for a while too?" "What makes you think that?" "Just a thought."

"To an extent, you are right about that." "I have not been looking for anything serious in the past few years." " I mean, that's not to say if someone came along that really blows my socks off I wouldn't consider it." "Hmmm!" "I mean you only live but once, and if that happens to be in the right place at the right time, then yes- Why not!" "Hmmm!" "So, how about this?" " This?" "Yea, this, Us, here and now." "Hmmm!" "Well you just never know, but to be honest, you're just traveling through Seoul." "Transiting!" "Yea, that's it." "I am staying for a little while, I have got my studies." "Yea I know." I added.

Dark glows from the outside. The street lamps shined in through the room. We sat, still sweating passionately, motionless. She said nothing, and I said nothing too. She is just warm enough for me. I could tell she was very comfortable being here with me. Free from her loneliness, I am also free from mine, the loneliness, although cautiously careful, not to get too comfortable being here. It will all be gone soon, fleeting like those other moments before. I hadn't garnered the courage to harness and make the most out of them, to be still and present.

She sat right there, in between the gap in my thighs, positioned in such as way that she sat like a Buddhist. She is on top of me and staring me down, almost as if she was peering into my soul. "I wonder what she's found down there? A little-lost boy still trying to make sense of the world, perhaps?" "I attempted to make sense of it, of the women I came across as I revolved around the question."

She stared me down like she held the keys to the questions I so desired to have.

The thrust began. She initiated. Once again I held her in order to keep her in place. Made sure her back doesn't greet the floor. Violently, the thrust carried on. She is doing most of it. I reminded myself to stay present this time. Her eyes closed firm, her lips smacked shut. She hummed and crooned underneath the hot Korean autumn breeze.

She humped and humped, yet I held her still, making sure her feet didn't kiss the ground. She wrapped them around my torso. Her intensity filled me with vigour as I listened to her groan. My silence didn't bother her. Her 24 years old peach bottom, soft and subtle. She made the most of her youth, thrusting like she is doing for sport.

I would help a little, just lift her, euphorically she glowed, it 's dazzled across her face. She is drenched in her sweat like a small flannel. I could only imagine how good she felt now. I am right there, right there with her.
She showed me just how easy it is to escape those dull, Sunday evening blues.

''Can you see?'' ''It's a bit dark in here.'' ''We ought to put some lights on.''

The blood had drained from my lower legs as I got up to switch the lights on. I almost slipped as I stepped on a film that lay on the wooden floor. It's one of Pat's Polaroid, one he had taken of her. She is smiling angelically in it. Like day and night, It contrasted sharply with images I had captured of her moments before, momentarily crooning.

Chapter 14

Late:

Wet rainy Manchester mornings. Not my favourites, not anyone's favourite. Not even professor Agata's favourite either. Half listened slumped into a bench. It's uncomfortable, technically, they were designed to be so. The audio from the small mic filled the room instantly with his small octave voice — something about Quantum theory and special relativity.

Jason arrived late. He peeked his head first through the large oak door. He checked to see if the coast was clear. A good 15 minutes behind the scheduled start time. There is huge certainty he is going to get caught walking in late. It's a huge part of the module, making up at least 60% of the required pass grade. He needed this, we all needed this module, and Professor Agata knew this all too well.

Cocky and brash, he exuberated a nonchalant sentiment — partly the reason why Jason was so cautious stepping into the hall.

Last warning, Mr. Washington ! If you arrive late to my class again, that will be the last of you. You can come in !

He announced on the small microphone, again his small octave voice quickly filled the room. Jason gently pushed open the door, cropped in like a night cat returning home at dawn.

Professor Agata, 54 years old, majored in Physics and Mathematical sciences Exeter doctorate. He was arrived for 15 years, with two children aged four and two. Frustrated!

Marriage on rocky grounds. Back sore from sleeping on his lounge sofa. The 4-year long turmoil had taken its toll on a once full of life man. He is bitter. He had trivialized her concerns for so long it had mounted, mounted to a good amount of emotional agony. It had changed him for the worse, too late for a reconciliation.

Jason walked in gingerly, shimmed through the role of sitting students, forcing them to put down their legs from the raised anchor they had created with the seats in front of them. They adjusted to give room and accommodated him as he wobbled through.

So, what perspective did Max Planck hold on the emission and absorption of light ? He asked.

The silence cuts through the class. It's early on a Monday morning. The look of glum on many faces.

I am referring to his views on electromagnetic energy. Anybody know? Any takers? He asked again.

Again a wave of silence swept overcomes the hall.

Planck's constant! The professor asked.

He scribbled on the blackboard behind him. It made a loud scratching noise as the microphone picked up as he scribbled fast.

"E" Energy equals to Planck's constant "h" multiplied by the frequency of the radiation "v"

"$E = hv$" was clearly written in the middle of the board for the class to see.

"You see, Planck hypothesis on energy emission could only occur in quantized form."

This lands deafly on the class.

That is, energy can only be a multiple of elementary units "hv", where "h," Planck's constant, is a physical constant, A quantum of action!

Physical constant! This held strong for me. Whatever is a physical constant? Jason whispered and I thought long about it.

A physical constant universal both in nature and time! He uttered through the small microphone.

I suppose it's just like love, universal in time and nature. A physical constant, the same regardless of colour, creed or disposition.

Agata was struggling with it. I struggled to find it. Jason was just about done with it. Oma had avoided it all together. It's elusive! In short, we were all late on it.

Theoretical like Planck's constant. You only imagine it to ring true. Now, here there lies the problem, long have I been phantom chasing.

Jason had nodded off. I imagined him having one those faraway dreams as he nodded off, deep in sleep. At least he is not going to have to listen to Professor Agata's stodgy disquisition. Perhaps, he is being accompanied by elephants. Just like Melanie whenever she deep sleeps. Again, it was quite late to be thinking of Melanie as several months had gone by.

General Relativity! We are talking about gravitation here folks, gravity as a geometric property of space and time. Does anyone know what a micro quasar is? The professor asked.

Again, the familiar silence returned to the hall, all 32.3meters of it. No one is uttering a word. Any takers? He asked. He returned back to his routine conjuring. Any? He asked again.

Well, they are astronomical objects that radiate an intense amount of radiation, and they exist as result of black holes ! Supermassive Black holes !

His mention of black holes described precisely how I felt. I found myself lost deep within one of these supermassive black holes Agata is rambling on about.

I suppose none of you read the brief before today's lecture? That will not be very good for any of you. He stated.

The tension returned to the hall, the silence now heavy in the air. The class realized how late they had been to not have read the brief before turning up to Agata's lecture.

''Someone should at least say something and save the day'' ''Save the class at least.'' I thought.

I debated whether or not I should take the fall for the class, but there was nothing there. I hardly understood quantum physics. Yes, it was a fascinating subject to study, but I hardly understood it. I am not sure any of us truly did.

Sir, to what degree of relevance does Planck's law have on a black body? And how does this affect a white body?

A girl from the front role finally broke the silence. What the hell is she talking about? Black body? White body? Oma muttered.

Jason off with a quiet snore. Those late night bar jobs might have had the best of him.

Well, first we have to define what a black body is? Excellent question by the way Charlene. The professor said. Thank you, sir! She replied.

A black body is an idealized physical body that absorbs all incident electromagnetic radiation regardless of frequency or angle of incidence.

Planck radiation describes thermal radiation dependant on the temperature of the body. The higher the temperature of the body, the more radiation it emits at every wavelength. He scribbled on the great big black board.

This was lost in the class, although Charlene seemed to muster the courage to engage with Agata. She nodded in agreement with his disquisition. She wasn't late like the rest of us. She was on time, and for once it made perfect sense what it meant to be on time and in tune.

So a black body, which absorbs all incident electromagnetic radiation at thermal equilibrium that is at a constant temperature, would emit electromagnetic radiation, also referred to as blackbody radiation, and does so according to Planck's law. It's radiation spectrum is determined by temperature alone, not by shape or composition. Interesting isn't it? He went on.

She nodded again as he scribbled on the board.

$Bv\ (T) =\ 2hv3$ 1

$C2$ ehv - KT

186

The class fell into a familiar dumb silence. No one seemed to want to engage with it: not the black body, not the Planck's and not Prof Agata.

Well, I will tell you all something. If you continue at this rate. You will all fail my module. You are all grown-ups, need to do your own research, and your own read up before my lectures. Read the brief! That's what they are there for. He uttered.

Like the last blow delivered by a championship boxer. It hit hard on the class. That Monday morning agony. ''*The poison of Agata.*'' We had all turned up late, even though the majority had been in the class way before the start time.

Chapter 15

Maria:

13: 45 pm Tarifa Spain 2014: Whenever you can, just simply let me know when you get here? She said.

Sure! I am just being held up, should be out in less than 30 minutes. I said.

Ok That works out perfectly.
Just at the store, what would you like for dinner? She said.

Being up in the air, seeing the clouds this high up in the skies, It's been quite awhile since I eyeballed them at this level. It's astonishing. A reminder of the joy and freshness of travel, a good 8 months had gone by since Budapest. We spoke at length over the phone since my return. She had been keen to rekindle as I was. With a look back, it had been the best moment of a spontaneous ten second decision made in a lifetime.

I caught her eyes as we brushed past on the walk pass the narrow hallway. I had no doubt had caught my glance by her sudden shift in posture as we drew closer and bumped shoulders.

3 hours at high altitudes of 34765 feet above sea level. That early dusk departure meant very little sleep could be had the night before. Jason and Oma had wished me well out of blind sighted encouragement; both were apparently still single. We would catch up in a week when they would push for all the details.

Laura's and Matthew's engagement date, my phone prompted me, it's on the 4th weekend to Halloween. The last to came through as we landed in Seville followed by Maria's.

It would be precisely 8 months since we all first met in Budapest. All of us were perfect strangers.

My small backpack was in the back compartment, that long hours drive to the coastal town of Tarifa endured under the glorious bask of the sun as I took the long windy roads to Maria. She had settled on the small surfer town in the south of Andalusia for its charm and the way it caught the light in the most dazzling of manner. It was beauty at first sight, just like when I first set eyes on her.

Those adjuring landscape of the south, brown and reverent to their lush green as I motored down their crisp tarred roads. They glistened on end, for hours perhaps, each attempting to cool the wheels with a splash, though the water had been in vain.

She stood at the red oak wooden door which had been aged drastically by the sun. She had done quite well in contrast. There she welcomed me in.

You are going to love it here. By the way. She said.

Spontaneity! The allure of subtlety, she is wondering and this can only be good.

Out came a bowl of freshly washed salad, diced with avocados as green as the fields I had just driven past, dark were the pickled olives she dazzled over like those tarred windy roads to sleepy Tarifa overlooked beautiful shorelines.

Quickly the room got filled with smoke from the oven that bellowed out of its door.

Sorry about that. She said. She seemed to be a lot more apologetic, a vast contrast to the girl I met a months back. She had been considerably dismissive then, now it seemed she just about agreed with me on everything.

So how was your flight in? And the drive? You must be exhausted? she asked as she tossed at the salad bowl continuously, as if waiting for something. *But, what?* I gathered she wanted me to say something or perhaps initiate some intimacy, she waited for something to happen, *but what?*

My ice breaker had been as stall as the moment it fell upon. I try at cooking. It will be a minute or so before the roast will be done. Are you hungry? She asked. A little. I said. Well that's good. She said.

She continued to toss at the bowl and the feta broke into smaller chunks.

Her lips bounded with mine. It would be our first in a long while since Budapest. She held on to me and the memories of the past came rushing as fast as the waves that crashed to shore.

The walk back that night, the push, her back against the wall on the corner of the ruined bar, all the memories came rushing back. She grabbed at my backside and squeezed hard. It all came back at me just like muscle memory, dormant until recessive.

 I learned that night, ''*She gave just as good as she gets.''* She shoved and pressed my back to a parked Chevrolet. I remembered it well, a small one, wet from the rain. I felt the instant soak from its panel as my shirt pressed upon it. It didn't bother me much.

She bit at my lower lips. The rhythm at which she went at it reminded me of track we played back at her apartment: "Miles in the sky." It took me right back to that time I bumbled along like the snares that rattled, her tongue rattled in my mouth. Her lips pressed against mine, thumped like the trumpet as she pressed. I simply let her do as she pleased. I watched as she took me, lost within the rhythm of her tongue like the snares.

As I pressed on her buttocks she leaned in to me even more. My shirt was soaked from the wet of the Chevrolet panel, but I cared little for this.
She turned to face the dimly lit street, narrowed and steeped with tall Vintage townhouses that lined them well as they took the corner that led out to the main square.

Where are you staying? She whispered into my ears.

Erm ! Well… The guest house. I said.

The thought of taking her back there hadn't crossed my mind. It wouldn't have been ideal, A shared room with three others, not the best of likely scenarios.

We can go back to mine. She remarked.

This quickly dissipated the anxiety. It had slowly crept up on me, as I thought of the three others. I was certain one of them snored, and not too well. That small single wouldn't have done well either.

Towards the square as we made our way through the dimly lit street. The tenderness of her palm, almost soothing as it rubbed against the inside of my hardened palm. She was searching for something, perhaps an approval.

She smiled as she caught a smirk on my face. *"The cat that got the milk."*

We take five more steps in addition to the previous ten, passing a small café. Its occupants were still in late at night, immersed in small chatters over bottled wine. With another massive kiss, the biting returned with her teeth pressed hard against my lips.

Small perks which she used to soothe her bites. A soft one here, another there, like the notes from a distant keyboard bumbled in the background, I could just about hear the saxophone played in the foreground.

We were back at the corner, barely a mile from Chevrolet we left behind. The dampness set heavy on my shirt and I still cared little about this. This time around, her back was to the wall. An old vintage townhouse, brown stoned with multiple of small ornate frescos carved onto one of its side pillars. My right hand drove through her smooth, silk-like hair. She pulled me into her with my shirt and held me with both of her hands.

In the same way, her tongue goes to work much more slowly, much more subtle to her previous vigorous bites. I followed with mine, making harmony like the keys to an organ, melodically communicated.

It's dim and reticent; I can only hear her groans as she kissed. I thought about pausing for a moment, gather on how far we had managed travel away from the ruined bar where Luca, Carlos, and David were surveying the talent underneath the Vineyard Arch. We were still nowhere near the square and its brightly lit concrete ground beaconed. The footsteps grew louder as they took the corner, I could hear them gradually building up. They belonged to two individuals, males, as I deduced from their heaviness, each hit the cobbled street with bits of stones dotted about. At times they kicked at the stones as they made their way towards the corner.

We should go. We can go back to mine. Maria suggested again.

She released me from her tongue and once again I found myself back at her rented apartment. Many miles from Budapest, many months from those moments and in warm tropics of Tarifa overlooked by the waves as they subtly crashed to shore.

She sat with her back to the window, opened for the fresh sea breeze to come in and partly to let the smoke out. The roast from the oven had now bellowed into the room. We had to let it out.

A perfect still as she sat gazed at the shores. She thought of something. It seemed heavy and I could tell. A perfect still like sketches of Spain I thought. Carefully guarded along- the sax soft and gentle. She had come a long way from home, Sao Paulo. Perhaps she missed it, perhaps not. It was difficult to say. She spoke little of the place since Budapest, like she had distanced herself from it, the distancing trombone on the piece we listened too — "Sketches of Spain".

We had been lost in each others' gazes, lost so we had forgotten the roast that the smoke alarm had to kick in to alert. She, a perfect still with a backdrop to the sea, loomed beyond the opened windows. She dashed and broke from it. A minute longer and it would have been better served to the street dogs that barked below us.

That was close. She said. It didn't get burnt, did it? I asked. No! It didn't. She said.

We were lucky. She said.

Lucky she said, *"But just how lucky were we really?"* I thought.

I mean, the possibility are what kept me going, in other words, hope. It's strange, you live your whole life in a city surrounded by people and never meet anyone you connect with. You go to the most unusual of places and meet someone in the most unlikely of circumstances, a fleeting glimpse. If you blinked, it could all have been gone in a flash.

We met at the ruined bar, but a slight hesitation on my part and we would not have been sitting next to each other's gaze, basked in the glorious Andalusian sunshine.

I wondered if many an opportunity presented itself to her, she could portray her talent well and shine. There, she was far from home: Sao Paulo Brazil. She seemed just as lost as I was. Beauty and fracas just as I was- Sketches of Spain.

The bumble of the drums returned. The floating Saxes whirled and I am deep in it again. This time my back to the rails, my gaze inwards to her flat. It's a collage of striking colours. I imagined this was an extension of her personality, striking shades of red. Blood red subtly conversed with hints of grass green, mud brown, mustard yellow here and there, earthy and vibrant. A sky blue sofa sat centre stage in the large white room. A lampshade was to the left of it, I wondered how much of this was hers.

She pressed at my lower side. I had become well accustomed too it. The pressure she exerted puts me at ease, it releases me in a way she had always managed to do, like masseurs. I returned the favour almost immediately and she is pleased, groaning to exhaustion with the same amount of pressure she had done seconds before.

The afternoon sun was kind on us. That cold early morning flight was a distant memory, basked in that glorious Spanish sun. It shimmered and I caught its glow on Maria's forehead, the way that she moved back and forth three quarters down below. It must all have been a dream, the way that she mentioned "We are lucky!" I am certain I am in luck, much of which I will have to repay her in good-turn.

I beaconed her to rise. Her back was to the rails as I mine had been earlier. I could witness the Spanish sun in all its full glory—euphoria as I enjoyed giving her pleasure much more than I had received it. She groaned just like the sketches of Spain. The waves from the sea crashed to shore as they moved in symphony with the way she moved her hips, wide and apart, with me down below. I was watching the waves, watching her.

The sky blue sofa was in the way. She almost took a fall, but I let her anyway so she does. She is spread eagle over its armrest, her back on the left of the cushion. She drew me in the same way she had always done. Mischievously, she stared, burning with something say, but I cared little about this. I am certain I knew what she wanted to say, like the keys to a composition, well rehearsed. Its player instinctively glides over the keys with no second guess. She was up in my arms and I ushered into her chambers.

The dance was on again, embarked on giant steps-Coltrane's "Cousin Mary" played on The Old Oliver plugged into her stereo, the very way I was also plugged deep into her. I gently evaded a hard land before we both take off. Her back hit her undone bed. My best guess was she rolled out of it in haste before receiving me. She once again was spread eagle, this time, her back to the ceiling. I watched and adored as she lay motionless like a Pythonidae minute from devouring a large prey.

We were back at it once again.

Chapter 16

Sunset:

15: 24 pm Haeundae Beach Busan South Korea: The sun shined at it's brightest since being in the city. It was mid-day as we laid bare in its element. Like a spit roast, I could feel the heat burning onto my skin. The shade provided little protection. My dark ebony skin glistened like a trophy as I lay next to her. She is enamoured by my presence.

The crowd was heavy on this summer's afternoon in Haeundae beach. I lay side by side with Aniko Lakatos, passenger K19, soaking up the sun's ray. She had reached out to me and I made the five hour long bus journey down to meet with her. She was equally pleased I made the effort. It's not that much fun traveling by yourself. She said.

It's our second day together since meeting on the plane: Cathy Pacific Flight CA972. She lay there radiant, her two boxer braids were gone. Her hair was loose, flying the course the wind gave it. She looked absolute tranquil.

I reflected back on my time with Eloise and what she had taught me in that short space of time of knowing her. She reached to pick up Pat's Polaroid of her from the ground. The same one that she had been smiling angelically in.

With all the will and intentions in the world, some connections just come to a short, abrupt, yet meaningful, end. She said at the time. We just simply need to move on. It's easier that way, for the both of us. She said. You give yourself the space to start over, start something new. Besides, we will be at opposite ends of the world. She said.

Our compatibility, refreshingly so as we shared an interest in the same sort of things, although not exacting to the point she was an absolute carbon copy of me. She had differences in opinions which made our conversation that much more interesting.

Aniko, on the other hand, was philosophical, intuitive and immersive sensitive. Take for instance her spill on Marlow's, the way that she saw society lost with not much social belonging.

A stage most synonymous with love! She said.

It is difficult to properly ascend to a healthy self-esteem with that kind of society. She went on.

My whole point is, you cannot be perfect, it is virtually impossible. She said.

We learn and ascend each pyramid level, as humanly possible, learning, re-learning and ascertaining, you know? She asked. I listened attentively as we both lay soaking up the sun's ray.

She continued. Until you can manage to ascend each pyramid level, I don't think you necessarily have to be an expert. Some levels are absolutely vital, like food and shelter, we need that of course. I listened as she spoke softly with a charm as captivating a spell.

Safety too! She added.

How about belonging and love? I asked her.

Of course, it is. That's why so many people are lost, lonely, and even worse, clinically depressed! She replied. We both lay flat in the sun, relaxed from its temperate outcry, yet having the most insightful of converse.

My point exactly, you can ascend through, even the more vitals of stages into belonging and love, with varied levels of achievement. She said.

Passenger *CA9245811* had me to a ransom. I had fallen deep within the depths of her. Each branch I held onto broke and I fell deeper.

There are people out there with no real friends but heck, do they have an enormous amount of self-esteem. She said.

Sharp as a tack as she was, it was difficult at times for me to entirely agree with her, the context of not needing to fully satisfy each level. Maslow's level pyramid seemed incoherent. Nonetheless, she had her opinion on it. Two good souls meeting at the pinnacle of a day's aubade, perhaps at the right time, perhaps the right place.

I let the sun work its way over my skin some more. It got cooler as the sea breeze gathered momentum and pushed inland onto Haeundae beach where Aniko lay, soaked up in it's rays. Her sunglasses glinted as she tilted her head from side to side and settled on a side facing towards me.

Are you okay? You seem awfully quiet today. She asked again. I am doing just fine, thank you, just taking it easy, that's all. I said Hmmm! Okay. She replied quietly.

Lost in my thoughts again, I thought of Maria. As it turns out she was a fleeting accord too. — that night at her apartment in Tarifa when she stood on the veranda overlooking the strait of Gibraltar. It's too early in the morning, early enough that none of the usual wind surfer's were up to catch the early morning drift.

You know, we can just about see Africa? She said. I think that could be Algiers, and that one, possibly Tunis in the distance. She said.

She pointed to the two bulging landmasses in the far distance, covered by the fog of the morning. I recollected her embrace from behind as she looked out onto the Strait. That warm thermal wind in the dark just before dawn. The twinkle of lights from the neighbouring buildings and some from the beach, illuminated from campfires set alight hours before, lit the night. She moved again in lateral undulation as she did back at the vineyard. Although this time, no music had been playing, just the wind whistling almost like careless whispers, gossiping to every local passerby. It carried her groans through every open window for every local nocturnal to listen in on.

It had all being a short momentous tryst, one I had expected to carry on for longer. I mean, she was just perfect. I hadn't considered what her needs really were, or if I met them. She spoke a lot about wanting to be free. "Free as a bird." The way that she had put it.

I mean the penny should have dropped then, and I mean that quite literally.

I know I want to see as much of the world as I can right now. She said. If I can pull it off, I'll travel for a lifetime, She said, for the rest of my life if possible. She said. There is a lot to see out there. She said.

You know, I couldn't be in a relationship with a guy if I couldn't make the time or care enough about him! She said.

I recaptured moments with her, her spread eagle
beaconing me in. That thin curtain that demarcated
between her bedroom and her living space oversaw
the strait. Free flowing just as she was a free spirit,
again I think she might have picked the place cause it
depicted so much of who she was, her personality,
her taste in colours. Those striking blood red were set
against grass green and mustard yellow. That great
sky blue sofa we waddled past, all had been an
absolute extension of her in living space.

I thought of Melanie. Many years had gone by and I
think I would not remember her again if we ever
crossed paths. Memories of her were long faded — a
distant past, one that had come with so much pain,
so much joy. It had come with much anguish for both
of us. We had to let go and fast. I had wanted to get
as far away from every single space and every single
setting we had once shared together. I yearned for
newness, but it had come at a cost. It had come with
many lessons too. I dare say we had a weird kind of
mythological exchange of lessons. Our stars weren't
aligned for long and they were not meant to be. We
both learned from the mess. I am much happier now,
much more in tune with myself laid bare in the
Korean pacific. There was no need to dabble, no need
to dabble in the hurtful of past memories now.

I thought of Jason and Oma — those good old days at
the dingy pool house south of Manchester. Jason at
25. You could see by the way he went at his job that
he preferred the surrounding of a dilapidated
construction site to social concuss.

He has a young family of his own, a proud husband. He's a dad to two lovely kids, a boy, four years of age, as dashingly handsome as his mom and a little girl, two years of age, the spitting image of her mom. There, I say, I was a tad jealous of that image of him, a photo he posted as a profile.

Well, Oma! He was living it up somewhere in the gulf, as I estimated he would. He did get engaged once, but later called it off. I guessed he got cold feet.

I thought of Matthew, how did he fare in his relationship with Laura? Theirs had been a serious one of a good number of months since that very trip to Budapest. I supposed it had worked out well for them — that warm Budapest evening, bonding with relative strangers over a cold bucket of Hungarian beer.

That's one good thing you soon learn from solo traveling. Matthew said. Other travellers naturally gravitate towards you like a moth to a flame. He mentioned.

MOD, as we all ended up referring to him. He told the most piteous of stories about the mental state of officers returning from the line of duty. At one time, the mood quickly took a turn, a downcast and empathetic feeling in the air as we listened tentatively.

He told us of being in convoy with the troops serving as a medical support on toll.

One particular officer who struggled badly with PTSD. He said.

It had left him pretty much suicidal. He mentioned.

This made my troubles seem relatively childlike compared to his stories.

One had a bad case of insomnia, staying up for days on end, not being able to sleep. He said.

He was dosed up on sleeping pills. They weren't going to be helpful for him either. He went on.

Another suffered really bad flashbacks, he woke up to a pool of night sweats. You would have thought he was doused with a bucket of water. He said.

The one most humorous. to say the least. was a marine officer with a history of sleepwalking — re-enacting orientations from his previous drill, complete with commentary. It got so bad, he once found himself in a swamp a few miles from his house, even the barks of his old terrier couldn't snap him out of it." MOD said of this particular officer.

The dog's bark alerted the neighbour, who jumped in to pull him out of it. he said.

He seemed to be at home with it all, just another day in a life of a MOD doctor.

That grateful evening with the most unlikely of strangers seemed to blossom into the most unlikely of relationships.

Are you okay Ray? I think you are a bit too quiet today! Aniko asked.

Ms. Lakatos, I said. I reached out for her left hand to hold onto. The Haeundae morning's sun had dimmed. Our fingers interlocked like we had done many times before then, only this time, there was a sense of security in her action. Her grasp like a mothering instinct that cared. Those flights, those sex, and those heartbreaks were put aside.

References :

- Overnight Travel series (Best Things to do in fukuoka)- Erwan Heusaff published YouTube 12th October 2016.

- Sapiens : A brief history of humankind, Extract : Map 6. The spread of Buddhism 2014 Yuval Noah Harari.

- Goodreads.com- Paula Acedo "Fools are those that believe smiles are a sign of happiness.

- Poet Author: Kissy Marie 2014 https://hellopoetry.com/Kissy-Marie/

Ray Decosta, a young man takes a succession of incidental travel flights. He is unassumingly on a quest, adrift equally in thought and motive, to find something, but what?

Each story draws from his past encounters, interwoven, delivered in an introspective thought driven manner. (T.P.W.M)

www.ingramcontent.com/pod-product-compliance
Lightning Source LLC
Chambersburg PA
CBHW031312120626
46554CB00001BA/379